MW00804762

MARY, handmaiden of the Lord

A

Biblically and historically

researched novel about

one of the most remarkable

women of all times

By

Virginia Nelle Wilson

Galaxy Books
Post Office Box 1421
Orange Park, FL 32067
904-264-0957
email: pmdelage@worldnet.att.net

First Edition
Publisher: Galaxy Books, Orange Park, Florida
Cover Design: Jefferson Rall
Production: Paul Delage
Editorial Assistance: Kathleen Delage

Library of Congress Catalog Card Number: 98-75191
ISBN 0-9652682-2-5

Dedication

I dedicate this book, *MARY, hand-maiden of the Lord*, to the memory of my mother, Lula Agnes Kuhn Phleger, who taught me to love and revere the words of wisdom in the Holy Bible. She encouraged my devotion to study.

This book and its soon to be completed companion, *MARY, mother of Jesus,* are the culmination of a lifetime of research. I regret that I did not get them finished in time for mother to read.

Virginia Nelle Wilson
Orange Park, Florida

Acknowledgments

My thanks are offered here for help given to me during the researching in the preparation of the writing of *MARY, handmaiden of the Lord.*

As I state in my preface I knew so little about the life and times of the Herod years I had to call on many people for advice and direction. I particularly want to thank Rabbi Gary G. Perras of the Beth Shalom Congregation of Jacksonville, Florida for his many hours spent enlightening me about the history and customs in that ancient land. I appreciate the liberal use of the library of the Congregation Ahavath Chased, the Temple, in Jacksonville.

Without the generous researching and editorial help from members of the United Methodist Church of Orange Park and friends representing various religious groups from the Jacksonville Branch of the National League of American Pen Women the project could not have been completed.

From the beginning this was not a retelling of a simple Bible story, this was the unraveling of the concept that a pattern was put forth that would in time change the world. Certainly the man Jesus influenced the world as no other single leader has. Critics say this man could not have come from lowly parents since he was obviously well educated in many areas. How did he acquire his vast knowledge?

Simply put, I believe that Mary was chosen for the task because she was a woman of great vision. We are still working on the vision held by her two thousand years ago. Equality was her goal.

Lastly I wish to thank my husband Jack for all his help in making these days pleasant study days.

PREFACE

Little is known about the Virgin Mary who bore and nurtured Jesus Christ. Her name appears in the Bible only nineteen times, yet she must have been a most unusual woman, selected for physical and spiritual beauty as well as for intelligence, integrity, and understanding.

Even after years of studying and teaching the Bible, my mental picture of Mary was ethereal. To me she was a holy and shadowy figure without the tribulations of daily human existence.

A Christmas lesson, prepared for my Sunday School class, aroused in me an empathy for the fourteen-year old maiden who lived in ancient Nazareth of Galilee, a strict and unyielding religious community where the penalty for adultery was death by stoning. The Bible relates the story that Mary experienced a secret, virginal pregnancy. I wondered if she suffered moments of fear that she, too, might be stoned since she was not married. When I learned that her cousin Elizabeth lived in Ein Karen, a four day trip by camel or mule over desert lands, I puzzled over how she could make such a journey alone.

I felt the need to put flesh upon this fragile Gospel skeleton. In volumes written about Jesus, I searched for moments in his life which He might have shared with His mother. I envisioned her as laughing, loving, crying, being angry, feeling hurt, and sorrowing. I wanted to picture the woman whom history has venerated but has failed to present as a real person experiencing the day-to-day drama of motherhood.

I spent four years of consecrated time researching and writing, weaving together historical, cultural, and religious lives of the Herod years. I was confronted with the problem of integrating into a continuous story the disagreeing chronologies and events of the four Gospels. I arbitrarily selected happenings where Mary very possibly was present.

I have tried to reveal a woman who shares motherhood joys and sorrows with the mothers of all the ages. I saw her as a woman uniquely modern for her time, who helped shape the life and mind of the child Jesus. I believe that she guided the man, Jesus Christ, and through Him she was a great influence in changing the status of women.

Her dreams of equality are being fought for two thousand years later. I honor her through this reverent, fictional biography.

Chapter One

Vengeance

Three young girls stumbled as they ran up the narrow cobblestone lane screaming, "Mary! They've got Rebecca! They're going to stone her!"

"Rebecca?" Mary cried out. She dropped the copper ewer and rushed to join her friends. The metallic clatter of the empty pitcher, bouncing from stone to stone, echoed behind the girls as they raced toward a frenzied crowd streaming up the narrow street ahead. Angry shouts resounded from the distant cliff.

She gasped for breath as the four girls neared the high ground that abruptly ended into nothingness. Mary had never been to this forbidden cliff. The place of death overlooked the vast Plain of Esdraelon, which stretched southward from Nazareth to the foot hills of Mount Tabor. Her family avoided that place where vengeance ruled, where people were stoned to death by neighbors and friends.

A trio of dogs charged toward the four girls, circling, darting in and out, barking and snarling at their feet. Ahead, Mary could see men churning about, their arms flailing as they talked, yelled and threw stones. Women were clustered in little knots, hanging back, away from the rabble of men whose fervid voices grew louder and louder. Bewildered children clutched their mother's robes. Whimpers and cries mingled with the steady hum of the women's voices.

The four girls stopped a short distance from a small cluster of women. They were clinging to each other, asking, "What is happening? Why are they stoning Rebecca?"

"No, No!" one of them shouted. "This is a terrible mistake. Only infidels are stoned!"

"Rebecca is not an infidel!" Mary cried out. "She loves *Adonai*. She sings for him at every festival. What could she have done to make these men stone her? She's only fourteen years old."

A sharp scream pierced the air. The four young girls hung on to each other. A strident voice rose above the rabble. It was Benjamin's. Mary was sure. Of course, it was Benjamin, the man to whom Rebecca had been betrothed for almost a year.

Then she saw him, towering above the others, looking like a mad man. A shock of wild gray hair burst free as his turban slid from his head. Protruding eyes and a livid scar, that sliced a barren streak through his gray beard, accented his flushed, pock-marked face. Dirt streaked, his robe was now loosened shreds of red and black brocaded silk flapping from a plaited golden cord tied about his over sized waist.

Stunned, Mary watched as Benjamin raised his arm to throw a stone into the area ringed with men. As rapidly as he could stoop to pick stones from the pile at his feet, he threw them, one by one, screaming all the while, "Harlot! Sneaking away to the stables with my worthless gardener!" He threw a fist-sized rock to emphasize his words.

Mary darted across the barren, clay space separating the clamorous men from the place where the girls and women waited. She stood on tiptoes and tried to peek over the shoulders of the cursing men but she could not see Rebecca. She bent down to peek through the narrow spaces between the moving men. Suddenly she heard the high-pitched wail, "Help! Help! Have mercy on me. *Adonai*, help me."

Mary knew that voice. She had no doubt. Rebecca was in the midst of that mob. Mary had to get to Benjamin. She pushed toward him, ignoring the sharp elbows jabbing her ribs, shoulders, and head. At last she was able to grab his arm and shout, "Stop. Stop. In the name of *Adonai* have mercy!"

Benjamin glared at Mary, his eyes wild, unseeing. He flung her aside, throwing her to the ground, where she lay sprawled and choking in the dust churned by stamping feet. Hurriedly she crouched into a ball to avoid being trampled. Tears welled in her eyes and spilled over her cheeks as she heard the rising chorus of voices shouting "Harlot! Harlot!"

Mary crept her way through the mass of legs and stamping feet, trying to find a place to rise, to escape. Suddenly stones pelted the area around her like a hail storm. One struck her shoulder and knocked her slight form to the ground again. Terrified, she struggled to her feet only to look directly into the contorted, flushed face of Rebecca's father.

"Stop them!" Mary screeched at him. "Stop them! In the name of *Adonai* save your daughter."

The man stared at her through glazed eyes. Mary, whose head barely rose above his elbows, clutched at his robe until the black silk ripped into wide ribbons, creating the effect of batwings when he raised his arms to beat the air with his fists.

A thick black and gray turban was askew on the top of his head. He was breathing heavily, panting with short bursts of air blowing through his thick lips. Rivulets of sweat ran down the channels in his cheeks and disappeared into his curly black beard. Heavy black eyebrows, knitted into a deep frown, creased his forehead as he glowered at the small figure attacking him. He shoved Mary aside and defiantly tossed a small rock toward the center of the circle.

Realizing this man was not acting rationally, she dropped the shredded silk and forced her way through the throng of men, pleading with each one. "Please stop," she begged over and over. "Can't you hear Rebecca's pain?" Each man ignored her, pretending not to hear.

Suddenly into the milling crowd a young man, wearing a rough homespun tunic, shoved his way through the sweat-drenched mob, pushing the men aside with muscular, tanned bare arms. Mary recognized the man whose black curly hair brushed his shoulders. Laban, the gardener. She had seen him as he worked about Benjamin's garden. Rebecca had taken her friends to see how much had been done toward building the private quarters she had insisted on having as a wedding gift. None of the girls spoke to the laboring man but they whispered to each other that they thought him to be very handsome.

Mary followed Laban through the crowd. She hoped that he could stop the madness. At the inner edge of the circle of men, Mary stopped suddenly. In the middle of a barren plot littered with stones lay Rebecca, bruised and bleeding. Her body was partially covered by a torn and blood-soaked yellow silk robe.

Laban fell to his knees beside her. "Rebecca!" he sobbed,

"Rebecca!" He cradled her in his arms. The wounded girl raised her head and cried out, "Laban!"

At that moment Benjamin's thunderous voice shouted, "Infidel! Son of Satan! You have sinned against the Lord, the God of Israel." Filled with fury he raged on, "I curse you for deflowering my betrothed." He lifted a large stone and heaved it toward the prone figures.

As Laban bent his body to shelter the crying girl the rock slammed into him, then another and another followed. Other men joined Benjamin's hysterical shouts. "Infidel!" "Death to Satan!" "Death to him who breaks the law of the God of Israel!"

Mary pushed her way toward the weeping, bleeding couple. An old man's rough, work-worn hands grabbed her shoulders. "Stay out of this or you'll get hurt," the man warned. She jerked free of his grasp. Again the rough hands grabbed her. The voice snarled through a snaggletooth grimace, "They broke the law. They knew she was betrothed to Benjamin. They knew the penalty for adultery. Stoning. That's what the law requires." [1]

Not only had Mary been stunned by the sight of her wounded friend, she was now bewildered by the word adultery. She recalled that sometimes Rebecca had blushed when she spoke of Laban, but she did not give a hint that he was her lover. No, she argued with herself. Yet it was true that Rebecca hated Benjamin and her father, too, for arranging the betrothal. She may have turned to Laban for solace.

Mary watched Laban struggle to his feet as he lifted Rebecca in his arms, shielding her from the stones as they smashed against him. Several of the men grabbed at him, tearing his clothing, ripping it from his body, pushing and shoving him toward the edge of the cliff where the ground dropped abruptly into a chasm.

When a large rock hit Laban on the side of this head, splitting it with the sound of thwacking a large ripe watermelon, he staggered backward, still holding Rebecca. Blood gushed over his face. He teetered at the edge of cliff for a moment and then the two blood-splattered bodies fell. Rebecca's screams echoed across the plain, then faded, stopped. Silence settled over the area until, as if quickened with new breath, the crowd surrounding Mary surged forward to the edge of the chasm to look down upon the two battered bodies.

Filled with a mixture of anger and despair she turned to face the men surrounding her and shook her fist at them as she cried out,

"She was my friend. What kind of men are you? Attacking a young girl! You are no better than the jackals of the desert!"

Frozen with the reality of what had happened, Mary felt a sudden and violent rush of nausea. Needing to get away, to run, to flee from this terrible place, she turned, stepped on a loose stone, and slipped forward. She struggled to keep her balance. For one dizzying moment the cliff—the men—Rebecca—the sun—all became a whirlpool. Fast-—faster—faster—everything—everybody disappeared into a mist. A man's hand grabbed her, steadied her.

Her feet were on the ground again. Her stomach still churned, and tears ran down her cheeks leaving salty bitterness on her lips. She pulled free from the tight grasp.

"I told you not to get into that mess," the old man said as he stepped aside. She elbowed her way back through the shouting throng, away from the violence, the vengeance, the madness of men filled with pious frenzy still unsatisfied. The shouts and the sounds of stones pelting the bodies at the foot of the cliff pounded in her ears.

Forgetting she had come with three friends she ran from the mob, past the knots of women and children until she dropped behind a stunted fig tree. She knelt and retched. Exhausted, she leaned against its trunk to rest, to gather the strength to get home, to get away from the terror that filled her. She wiped the soured bitterness from her lips with the back of her dust-covered hand leaving clay-brown streaks across her face.

The mob was moving away from the cliff, breaking up into small groups, moving toward her. They were leaving Rebecca and Laban to rot at the bottom of the cliff, going on as if nothing had happened. Mary wondered, *How could Benjamin, the betrothed, and Nathan, the father, do this? How could they believe that Adonai demands such cruel, inhuman punishment for two young people?*

Mary scrambled to her feet, afraid of the approaching men. She raced home as if she were being chased through some alien land by an unseen monster. She could not erase from her tear-blurred eyes the sight of Rebecca's bleeding body, could not deaden her mind to the sound of the rock splitting Laban's skull or shut out the shouts still vibrating in her ears.

Chapter Two

The Law

Heat waves shimmered from the sun-baked cobblestones as Mary ran between the rows of white-washed wattle and daub houses.

For her, all the joys of that early springtime morning had vanished. The joy of the unexpected summer warmth, the budding of flowers, the clear blue sky, and her thoughts of her betrothal to Joseph had left her mind. The Nazareth she had always loved, the Nazareth of happiness and beauty, was changed forever. Now it seemed cruel and ugly.

With her long, blonde hair loosened, she clutched the blue scarf around her neck, grateful she had not lost it when it slid from her head. Perspiration webbed curls over her forehead. Dust and tears smeared her cheeks. Dark splotches stained her pale blue robe.

"Home," she panted with shallow breaths. "If I can only get home nothing can harm me."

With a rush of strength, she reached the small house which resembled every other house along the way. She pushed aside the heavy wooden door and darted in. Blinded by the sun's glare, she paused in the sudden darkness and leaned against the wall while she caught her breath.

In the cool, shadowy room her mother knelt before a low table, kneading a puffy, round ball of dark dough on a worn, wooden board. Anna looked up and said,

"Mary! What happened?"

Sobbing, her body trembling, Mary dropped to her knees beside her mother. Anna quickly wiped flour from her hands on a worn, striped cloth tied about her waist.

"Tell me, my child, what's wrong?" she asked, smoothing Mary's tousled hair. "Your robe is soiled. Your face is dirt streaked," she said as she touched Mary's cheek. She held her daughter's face between her hands, then wiped the tears from the girl's eyes. "Tell me. Where have you been? Are you hurt?"

"At the cliff . . . , " Mary shuddered.

"The cliff? What . . . ?"

"A mob stoned Rebecca. She's dead," Mary sobbed.

"Your friend, Rebecca?" Anna asked as Mary's father, Joachim, appeared in the doorway, leading from his workshop in the rear. Mary and her mother did not see him as he paused to kiss the tips of his fingers and lift them to the small box on the right hand side of the doorway. They did not hear the familiar murmuring of words, "Hear O Israel; the Lord Thy God . . . . " The remaining holy words ran on so fast they were unintelligible until the last few ". . . with all your soul, and with all your might." [1]

Joachim was tall and muscular. His dark, full beard glistened with touches of silver and his thick black hair was neatly plaited into two fine braids in front and back of each ear. A craftsman's chip of wood nestled behind his right ear. He wore a brown, homespun robe flecked with wood shavings. The robe was cinctured with a wide leather girdle from which hung several small tools. He was hand-polishing a small piece of wood as he stepped into the room and asked,

"Did I hear you say there was a stoning this morning?"

Mary and her mother turned toward him as he asked his question. "Yes, Father, a mob stoned Rebecca!"

"You remember Rebecca, Mary's friend, " Anna said. "Her father, Nathan, has a silk market on the Street of Bazaars."

Joachim nodded. "Wasn't she betrothed to the rug merchant, Benjamin, some time ago?"

"Their wedding was to be at the next full moon," Mary's voice trembled. "I saw her stoned to death, Father. I saw it. I'll never forget her screams. Or the blood. She screamed and begged for mercy but the men wouldn't stop," Mary sobbed. Putting both hands up to her face, she leaned against her mother's ample breast.

Anna soothed the girl's heaving shoulders while motioning for Joachim to let the girl cry. After a while Mary looked up at her father,

"They had no right," she sobbed. "Those men had no right . . . they were like wild animals snarling over dead carcasses. That fat old

Benjamin, and even her own father, threw stones and shouted." Tears ran down her cheeks. "A large rock hit Laban's head and split it, then he and Rebecca fell over the cliff's edge. Even then the crowd didn't stop. They kept throwing larger and larger stones, shouting horrible words."

"Laban?" Joachim asked. "Who is Laban?"

"Rebecca's friend. He broke through the crowd and threw his body over hers to take the rain of stones . . . ."

"Was he Rebecca's lover?" her father cut in.

"I don't know. But even if he were, those men had no right," Mary shook her head.

A pair of brown goats nosed into the open doorway, sniffed the rich odor of Anne's kitchen, then bravely set their slim hoofs over the door sill. Anna slid the striped cloth from her waist, and snapped it at the intruders. The goats backed away, bawling their protests as they trotted back along the narrow cobblestone lane.

Joachim cleared his throat several times, then asked, "Rebecca was betrothed to Benjamin, was she not?"

Mary and Anna nodded.

"Then, I say, that if Rebecca and this young man Laban broke the law . . . if Benjamin . . . caught them breaking the law . . . there could be no disregarding the word of *Adonai* without paying the penalty."

"It's all her father's fault," Mary said. "It was inhuman to espouse Rebecca to a man old enough to be her father. Her father should have been stoned for ruining her life."

Anna said, "Mary, my dear, she ruined her own life. She could have had everything she wished for in a few weeks, when she became Benjamin's wife."

Mary stood, looking first at her father and then her mother, and answered, "The thought of having to kiss that man made her sick. I don't blame her. What kind of a life would it be for a young girl like Rebecca?"

"Evidently her father thought it was a good match," Anna spoke slowly, wiping her hands on her apron. She returned to her bread-making, sprinkling brown barley flour over her hands before plunging them into the round ball of soft dough. "Benjamin lavished everything on that girl," she went on. "I heard he was having a room on the top of his house built because she wanted a private space of her own."

Mary looked down on her mother's hair drawn tightly into a large soft roll at the nape of her neck. Mary noticed for the first time the little strands of short fluffy hair that grew below the large knot far down on her mother's neck. A ray of sunshine fingered its way through the door to trace a bright line across her head. As silver threads glistened here and there through the glowing copper strands, Mary thought, *My mother is getting old, she doesn't understand how a young girl feels about marrying an old man.*

"Yes," Mary said, while staring at her mother's hair. "I'm sure her father thought it was a great match." She walked to the door, looked in the direction the goats had taken, then turned back toward her parents. Lifting her chin high she said, "And the bride price was high! Her father was guilty of selling her into the slavery of a loveless marriage."

"Bah, what is love, anyway?" Anna gave the dough an added slap with her palm. "Not necessary."

"Your mother speaks the truth. Love comes after marriage."

Mary stood silhouetted in the doorway. "But not with an old man." She struck the wall beside the door with her fist. "What about the law that says a girl does not have to marry someone whom she doesn't like? How does the law protect a girl from a greedy father?"

"I suppose her father knew that the young man you call Laban was totally unacceptable as a husband. What does his family do? Where do they live? I've never heard the name about town."

"He was Benjamin's gardener."

"A gardener!" Anna gasped. "These two shouldn't have been speaking to one another, let alone talking about being in love."

"A man couldn't allow such rabble to be a part of his family!" Joachim said. "Being an important merchant, it would be unseemly for a father to give his blessing to his daughter's marriage to a man far below her social standing. There are few men who can match Nathan's importing business."

Mary turned to her father. "Status . . . status," she said. "Can gold and silver buy everything? Is money and status all you men think about?"

"Do you think Jacob and I were not thoughtful when we espoused you to Joseph, my Daughter?" He placed the small piece of wood he held in one hand on the top of a small chest by the door and walked into the center of the room. "It is now six months since your official betrothal. Do you think we men were thinking only of status and money when we planned all this twelve years ago?"

"Not money, Father. Carpenters are never wealthy. Status, yes. You and Jacob wanted to be sure neither of your children married beneath you."

"No! We were thinking of your security and Joseph's. Your mother and I felt safe knowing Joseph's family would care for you in case something happened to us while you were still a child. Don't say money and status are all fathers think about."

"But, you had no idea if Joseph and I would be suited to each other. Fortunately we have been blessed. Joseph and I love each other. That is why I felt so sorry for Rebecca, sentenced to a living death with an old man."

"You keep calling Benjamin 'old.' He is not so old . . . maybe he has lived a few years more than I and is a bit heavier." Joachim shrugged his shoulders, straightened his body to its full height and pressed his rounded shoulder back to emphasize his own work-hardened figure. "He's a young man yet. Lost two wives and now needs a mate."

"What of a betrothed man who breaks this law? Would he be stoned also?" Mary raised her chin high, lifted her eyebrows slightly and looked directly into her father's eyes. "What of Benjamin? Has he not lain with women? Did anyone ever think of stoning him?"

Shocked by Mary's question, Anna stopped kneading the bread and looked up. "Mary," she scolded. "You should show more respect for your father . . . asking about . . . about . . . ?"

"It's all right, my Wife. I will answer my daughter's question so that she may know the reasoning behind the law. Benjamin probably did hire harlots who make their livings by selling their . . . ah . . . services. There have been women like that . . . well . . . I suppose you could say forever. These women have no thought of marriage or birthing legitimate heirs. But the womb of a man's wife is sacred to him. A betrothed woman who has given her body to another man could be carrying that man's seed into the marriage bed. A husband has a right to be assured his first born, his heir, is of his own seed. Do you understand? A man has a right . . . ."

"But does he have the right to kill her for betraying him? Kill her by stoning? Is there no forgiveness in a man's heart for a woman? I saw Rebecca's own father throwing rocks."

"He will probably regret that one day, but today, he was filled with the shame his daughter had brought upon his family plus he will have to pay back all the bride price money . . . and he probably doesn't have it any more. He may have invested in merchandise for his bazaar. Nathan may be facing financial ruin. No doubt he feels the loss of the townspeople's respect, as well. Ruin is a terrifying state for a man." He raised both hands and shook them above his head.

"Would you stone me, Father"

"You would never break the law, Mary. I would never have to make that decision. You are a good girl, brought up with love and fear of *Adonai*. There is no young woman more pure and perfect in all the land, Mary."

"I ask you again, Father. Could you stone me?" Mary placed her hand on his arm. He looked down at the small fingers pressing on the sleeve of his work tunic and moved his right hand toward them, paused and then, waved as if dismissing the thought as ridiculous.

"There is no need to answer that question. You would never break one of our God's commandments, Mary." He turned from her, picked up the partially burnished piece of wood from the chest by the door, kissed the fingertips of his own right hand, touched the mezuzah and left the room, mumbling his holy words. Soon the thud of mallet striking wood drifted from the workshop.

"Mary, women don't question the law," Anna said. "They just obey it. It's hard being a woman, especially a mother, for she sees things which do not seem to be fair. She worries about her children's future. Rebecca's mother was not at the cliff, was she?'

"I didn't see her—but the crowd was churning so—and there were so many people."

"She wouldn't be there," Anna said, shaking her head slowly. "A mother is a mother forever, no matter what her child does."

"Her mother knew how Rebecca felt about Benjamin," Mary said.

"She disapproved of the engagement but her protests were over-ruled by Nathan."

"If she knew or even suspected that Rebecca was not keeping her betrothal vows, it was her duty to insist that the girl obey. There is no excuse for breaking a holy decree. *Adonai's* law is first, always."

Mary's voice rose, "Yes! *Adonai's* law is first but we must remember that it is men who put meanings into the words. They bend the law to fit their own needs. You know that!"

"I know," her mother answered softly. "But that's the way it has always been in our land, Mary. We are *Adonai's* chosen people We obey his commandments. Always. He has been good to us and we must thank him every day. He has promised a Messiah to lead us to the glory that was David's. When that time comes the whole world will know that Israel's *Adonai*, our one god, reigns."

"Mother, I, too, pray for the day when our blessed Messiah comes to deliver us from the Roman heel. Each day I thank *Adonai* for my loving family and for Joseph. He will be a wonderful husband."

"And father, if you are so blessed."

"Yes, if we are so blessed." Mary's face flushed and she cast her eyes down.

"Where did you put the water jug, Mary?"

"I must have dropped it. I was so upset about Rebecca. I'll go back and get it now."

"First, go change your robe and wash your face."

Mary touched her mother's cheek with her lips before she left the room.

Chapter Three

Gabriel

Mary retied a fresh scarf about her hair as she stepped into the brilliant noonday sunshine. This time she walked slowly along the quiet street. The sun bore down making the air seem too hot for early spring. It was the time of day when most people were indoors, out of the heat, doing quiet chores. Occasionally a child, eating a crust of bread or a piece of fruit, would stand to watch her as she walked by. In the distance she could hear the shouting that had frightened her earlier that morning. She was tempted to go back to the bluff but she knew there was nothing she could do to help Rebecca. It was too late. She found the ewer where she had dropped it beside the cobblestone street. She picked it up and continued on her way along the well-worn footpath to the well which was used daily by most women and girls who lived in Nazareth. At the city-gate she paused to enjoy the beauty of the land just outside the walls. Recent rains had turned the drab desert into a land of color. Masses of purple and rose anemones, mingled with splashes of yellow mustard, brightened the sand and rocky landscape. For the first time that morning she noticed that the sky was as blue as the flax blooming in the fields. However, all this beauty made Mary sad as she realized that she and Rebecca would never share this scene again.

Mary had not thought about death before that morning's tragedy. She wondered, *Who will take care of Rebecca's and Laban's bodies? Surely some of the relatives or close friends of Rebecca's parents will. My mother was one of the seven friends who prepared Joseph's mother for burial and wrapped her body in the white linen winding sheet.*

Joseph was so grateful for the tenderness of the women and for the strength of the pallbearers who carried the shrouded body on a plank to the burial cave. My father was one of those pall bearers.

I remember how Joseph and his father walked immediately behind the body and the couple's other children and grand-children followed. I walked with the women behind the men in the procession, ahead of the paid mourners who continued a steady mournful wail which echoed back from the hills.

Joseph and his father, in addition to all the cousins of both sides of their family, were still in deep mourning for the woman, who had died soon after Mary and Joseph's betrothal six months ago. Ruth had been ill for some time. The two families were happy that she had lived to attend the *giddushan*. That party that had been anticipated for years. They had awaited Mary's blossoming into womanhood so that Joseph might formally ask Joachim for Mary's hand.

Mary smiled as she recalled how the two fathers had traced their ancestries: Jacob from the house of David, Joachim out of the family of Levi. They were pleased to have the opportunity to recite their family lineages. Mary reminded herself, *I must remember to ask Father to recite his and mother's line of forebears for me again. After all, it will be up to me to remember for my future family. Sometimes "who begat whom" becomes lost in the sing song of my mind.*

I wish that I knew how to write. It doesn't seem fair that only boys can go to the synagogue school to learn to read and to inscribe letters. Girls have to memorize everything about holiday customs and all the food laws. We're not even taught how to keep a written record. I guess it seems more important for a girl to learn to loom fine fabrics, to embroider, and to cook meals according to the Law. Besides, it would take a girl away from household duties to spend hours practicing writing. I am very grateful that Father taught me to read the Torah as carefully as he would have taught his first born son.

She thought about Joseph and his father, *They have no woman to care for them. Men seem so helpless when doing plain household tasks. I've made plans to change the house, make it more colorful, more cheerful. I'm anxious to see the bright cloths I have loomed for the table that Joseph's father made for his bride many years ago. The wood still has a beautiful glossy patina. They should look good with all the bright pillows I've made to place around the rooms. I am so anxious to start housekeeping.*

It will be fun living with Joseph—and his father. I just know he will want to stay with us. Joseph is the youngest of the family. All of his brothers and sisters have moved from the family circle and are raising families of their own. I don't mind. Joseph's father is a dear old man—much older than my own father. He doesn't talk much and I'm sure he will never interfere with our lives.

Mary walked in the shade of olive trees edging the lane. Just around the bend was the big plane tree where women usually gathered while coming and going to the well. There they rested a moment or so—to cool off—and to exchange gossip. Since it was noon most of the women had gone home, out of the heat. But a few clustered there, talking. One of them called, "Mary, I saw your water pitcher down the lane. Did you forget to take it home this morning?"

"Yes, I was so upset over Rebecca's stoning I ran home to tell Mother and didn't think of the jug."

The women huddled to listen as one of the older women remarked, "Too bad about Nathan's daughter. But then she knew . . . ," the woman lowered her voice to a whisper, "I understand she was in . . . the family way. Benjamin had never touched that girl . . . he swore he didn't . . . even though he had the right . . . being betrothed and all."

Mary didn't say anything. *There is no need to try to change these women's minds*, she thought. *They are too old to ever expect or to want love in marriage. How lucky I am to have Joseph. We are blessed for surely a marriage built on love will be better than a marriage with one partner detesting the other.*

Mary left the little knot of women and went up the worn path toward the well. Ahead there was a sharp bend around a huge boulder, which was the beginning of an overhanging outcropping of wind-worn sandstone. From there the path went uphill all the way to the well where fresh water gushed from rock. Moisture from its steady flow maintained a garden of wild flowers whose colors changed as different varieties budded, blossomed, and went to seed. Across from the huge boulder a patch of red lilies, rich chalcedonicum lilies, were in bloom. Mary stooped to look at the perfectly formed trumpet-shaped flowers so regally poised on tall green stalks. A rich scent, smelling as sweet as myrrh, filled the air. Mary breathed deeply of the fragrance.

Mary thought, *Truly these are the flowers Solomon praised in his Book of Songs. It seems that the sun shines brighter on the lilies than it was while I was walking on the path. It seems like lightning is flashing.* Mary looked up and saw an ethereal figure standing in the walk. She knew it was an angel even though she had never seen one. *I know that is an angel. I know because I've heard about angels of the Lord since I was little. I've heard the rabbi read about them from the Holy Scrolls. There it is—a body—yet not a solid body—a body of light really. The features of the face could be that of a man or a woman. The blue eyes seem to pierce me.*

The angel spoke with a soft voice,

"Hail, O favored one, the Lord is with you.

Blessed are you among women."

Mary was too weak with fear to rise, so she knelt in among the red lilies as she looked up to the shimmering white figure before her. Her voice trembled as she asked, "Who are you?"

"I am Gabriel, who stands in the presence of God.
Do not be afraid, Mary, for you have found favor
with God. And behold, you will conceive in your
womb and bear a son, and you shall call his name
Jesus.

"He will be great, and will be called the Son of
the Most High; and the Lord God will give to
Him the throne of his father David, and he will
reign over the house of Jacob for ever; and of
his kingdom there will be no end." [1]

The calm, quietness of the angel's voice cast a hypnotic spell over Mary. Wonder and consternation mesmerized her. Summoning courage to keep her voice steady she timidly asked, "But how can this be since I have no husband?"

"The Holy Spirit will come upon you, and the
power of the Most High will overshadow you;
therefore the child to be born will be called holy,
the Son of God. And behold, your kin, Elizabeth
in her old age has also conceived a son; and this

is the sixth month with her who was called barren. For with God nothing will be impossible." [1]

Mary knew the legends of the promised Son of God. The Messiah was a topic of daily conversation in all Jewish homes. A king was coming to lead their people just as, centuries before, Moses had led them through the wilderness.

A warm hallowed fervor swept over her. Softly she said, "Behold, I am the handmaid of the Lord; let it be to me according to your word." [2]

She bowed her head. "But I am a lowly peasant girl; surely the Lord will want a royal maiden to bear His Son."

She looked up and Gabriel was gone.

Mary remained kneeling. She wondered what had happened to her. *Did I really see an angel or was I overcome by the heady fragrance of the lilies and the hot noonday sun?* She relived the brief encounter with—he said he was Gabriel. She wondered if she had fallen asleep—surely she had been dreaming. She felt exhausted. She reasoned, *Seeing the stoning of Rebecca has been a terrible experience which has unnerved me. I was walking, thinking about the morning and the beautiful flowers. Let me see, I had stooped to look at these red lilies. Perhaps I fell and hit my head on a stone.* She touched her chin and forehead with her fingers and felt no soreness. When she stood she saw the stains from the crushed lily petals streaked over her blue dress. She tried to brush the red away and her hands smeared the dusty red pollen. She turned homeward. *Why did the One God, the Lord, chose me?*

As if she were in a trance she walked slowly and pondered that question. *In the temple the priests talked of the Messiah and said he would come to save the nation—their beloved Israel—from the crushing oppression of the Romans; a Messiah to destroy the power which sought to deny the freedom of Yahweh's chosen people. The Prophet Isaiah had foretold that a virgin would bring forth Immanuel. He had called the Son Immanuel—not Jesus.* Then she questioned again. *Why me? I am not of royal blood to bear a king.* Surely the Lord's messenger would not have made an error.

Then she knew! *I have been chosen! Out of all the maids the Lord has selected me for that honor.* She began to run down the path. *I must tell Mother everything that has happened. The Son of God! She will be pleased that the family will be so honored. She'll probably already know. Gabriel will have told her by the time I reach home.*

She ran down the path past the plane tree. The women had left its shade and she saw them ahead of her, turning into the cobbled pavement. She was glad they were gone before she had to pass them. She didn't want to explain how her robe had become soiled. They wouldn't understand why she was kneeling in among the lilies. She ran by the houses she had sauntered past earlier. She was unaware of the heat that dampened her hair into tight curls about her forehead and cheeks. Her face was flushed and thin wisps of dark gold hair clung to the nape of her neck.

When she entered her house Mary did not see her mother standing with her arms akimbo but she knew from the sharpness of her voice that her mother was displeased.

"Mary! What is the matter with you? Again you come rushing in like an infidel—not bothering to bless the door with your greeting. And where is the water jug? Have you broken it and are afraid to tell me?"

"No. I haven't broken the jug but I have something to tell you."

"Tell me nothing! Get back and bring home some water—or should I send Salome after it? How do you expect me to prepare our evening meal? Your father will be finishing up his work soon and will need water for his evening ablutions. How can you be so irresponsible?"

"Irresponsible?" Mary bowed her head. This was not happening at all like she thought it would. *Gabriel has not told my mother the wonderful news. Maybe I did dream it after all.*

"Yes. Being irresponsible is not like you, Mary. Are you sick? Let me feel your forehead." Her floured hand left a white streak on the girl's wet skin. "No fever. You're warm from running—warm and covered with perspiration. And look at you. You come home for the second time this morning with your robe dirty and stained."

"On my way to the well," Mary said in a quiet voice. "I fell at the bend in the lane."

"By the outcropping boulders?"

Mary nodded and added, "Where the red lilies grow." Just telling where she had fallen made her recall the awesome brilliance of Gabriel. She remembered the warm, loving surge which had enveloped her at the same time.

"What will people think, seeing you so unkempt?   You are a woman not a little girl. Now you go change immediately,"

Mary went into the little space curtained off from the main room which she and her sister shared. Through the drapery she heard her mother's voice continue, "Yes, I know the place. That path is steep and slippery with many rolling pebbles."

As Mary dropped the soiled blue robe about her feet and pulled a fresh one about her she said, "I was not looking where my feet stepped. I will be more careful next time."

She looked at the red flower stains and knew they would have to be soaked in cold water. She went out into the small patio area for an extra pitcher and hurried away without saying goodbye. Mary heard her mother calling to her sister, Salome, to go along with her. She thought, *To ensure the return of the water pitcher.* Mary ran so that she would be too far ahead for the younger girl to join her. *Irresponsible, indeed! Just wait until Gabriel does tell Mother of the great honor the Lord has bestowed upon her family.*

Chapter Four

Mary s Burden

Mary did not linger along the deserted pathway. The evening shadows seemed to lengthened all the trees and shrubs into long-legged black creatures. The plane tree was but a dark blur. Hesitantly she approached the corner where the road curved around the boulder cliff. Her mind whirled. *What had happened? Did I imagine it all? If my meeting with Gabriel really did occur—how can I explain my being with child? Why didn't Gabriel tell my mother? How can I tell her? Will she believe me? Surely Adonai will announce it for me some way.*

She tried to think how the Lord's booming voice would say, "I, Yahweh, announce that Mary is bearing the Messiah!*" Yes, He will tell everyone and they will all love His child. I needn't be afraid. The Lord will show me.* Her heart began to pound. *But what if He doesn't? What will I do?*

She relived the morning hours with the screaming rock-throwing crowd. "O, Rebecca. They killed you," she cried out. "Lord help me. They will kill me too."

She hurried on into the gathering shadows. *I must not worry,* she thought. *When I see Joseph he will know what I should do. I'm sure Gabriel told him since he will be sharing the raising of God's child.*

She came to the patch of red lilies and touched the moist, smooth petals. She said to the flowers, "You are my only witnesses. I know I did not dream Gabriel's visit. He said I would be carrying God's child but who will believe that I am still a virgin?"

A gentle breeze stirred the lilies. A heady fragrance engulfed her. A white dove fluttered near the flowers then flew over the narrow uphill path. Mary ran all the way to the well, tied the rope on the handle of one pitcher and filled it, and filled the second one. She lifted them to her shoulders and hurried back toward Nazareth.

In the distance Mary saw pale lightning flashes behind a cloud and two ladders of sunshine streaking down from the sky. No longer frightened, she believed that she had witnessed a sign from God telling her that He would take care of her. She bolstered her new found strength by singing one of David's Psalms all the way home.

> "I will extol Thee My God, and King
> And bless Thy name for ever and ever.
> Every day will I bless Thee.
> And praise Thy name for ever and ever.
> Great is the Lord and greatly to be praised;
> His greatness is unsearchable." [1]

She was euphoric by the time she reached her home. She stopped by the door, kissed her finger-tips, touched the mezuzah and said a prayer as she stepped over the doorsill.

"It's about time," her mother called out. "You certainly could have saved yourself a lot of trouble if you had thought a little instead of being so irresponsible."

That word again!

Her mother went on, "Here, give those to me."

She took the jugs so quickly water lapped over the edges, splashing two wet spots on Mary's robe. Mary flinched slightly as the cold wetness spread over her shoulders. Even though she carried water every day her arms ached from holding both of them in the carrying position for so long. She rubbed feeling back into her muscles as she went into her room.

"I didn't realize you were bringing back two ewers, Mary. I tried to get Salome to go with you, but by the time I found her you were out of sight."

"I had to bring extra to wash my soiled dress," Mary said as she poured water into a bowl and doused the lily-stained robe into it. She rubbed at the red spots but they were stubborn and left the material patterned with lavender tracings. Realizing further rubbing would be futile she draped the robe on the young almond bush at the back door. Her mother had taught her that dew and sunshine would bleach stubborn stains. She hoped that it would work this time.

Mary dried her hands and joined her mother in the preparation of the evening meal. She was careful to keep all utensils and dishes separated as specified in the Jewish laws. No one ever told her why milk products should not be on the table with, or cooked with, meat. Someday she planned to ask her mother to explain all the complicated dietary rules, but, certainly not at the moment. It was obvious that Anna was already provoked with her forgetting the water jugs two times in one day.

Mary tried to act as if nothing unusual had happened. She wanted to give her mother another opportunity to talk with her. As she moved about the room she tried to speak in a casual tone but her heart and mind were racing. When she could wait no longer she asked,

"What about the Messiah our people are waiting for?" Her mother poured water in a basin then set it out in the late sun saying, "There. That should be warmed by the time I have your father's evening meal prepared. What did you ask me, Mary?"

"What about the Messiah our people are expecting"

"The Messiah? Why do you ask?"

"Just curious. Is the new king to be born to royal parents or will he be born to a peasant, perhaps?"

"Certainly it will be to a very special woman—foretold to be a virgin. I understand at Mount Carmel they have a school near the great salt sea for about a dozen or so girls where they are in training to be the mother of Immanuel, as the prophets call him. [2] I don't know how they are chosen but no doubt they come from their own little exclusive group, Essenes, I think they call themselves. I don't understand about them but your father was talking with some men at the temple one day. They seem to think that the Essenes are religious fanatics who preach that they are establishing the world for the prophet Elijah who will be coming soon with the Messiah. The rabbi says that we should ignore them. He says few people take them seriously. They're too radical. Is that what you wanted to know, Mary?"

"I just wanted to know if anyone knew who the mother of the Messiah would be."

Joachim appeared at the door from his workshop. Before he spoke he touched the prayer box on the door and paused to repeat his blessing. He turned toward Mary and said, "What's this your mother tells me about you being so rattlebrained you can't remember to bring home the water jug?"

"Nothing, Father. Nothing. I'm sure that I have been too upset about Rebecca to think clearly. I'm sorry if I caused your meal to be late." She bowed to her father and then to her mother.

He waved his hands over her as if giving a benediction, "We forgive you, Mary, but try to remember that you can't take on the worries of everyone. It's enough to live your own life in God's way. Peace be with you."

She bowed her head and murmured, "And with you, Father."

Mary and Anna prepared the dinner while Salome gathered the boys and watched to see if they washed themselves properly. With the evening preparations completed the family seated themselves on cushions about the low table and ate the food that Anna and Mary had cooked. When they had finished Joachim wiped his beard with his hand, looked about him, nodded to the younger son and said, "David, it's your turn to say grace in praise of our Lord."

"Yes, Father," the lad said, bending his head until his chin pressed against his neck. The six year old's voice rattled speeding words with a sing-song cadence, "Blessed are You, O Lord our God, King of all the world, who gives food to all the creatures of the world, Blessed are You, Oh God, Giver of food to all." [3]

The boy started to rise when his father touched his shoulder to keep him seated. "That's very fine that you learned the words so well, David, but you did not think as you said them. You sounded like a magpie. Our Lord wants to hear and I want to hear you say that prayer with meaning for every word. We are thankful for our food. The Lord is the Giver."

Chastened, David slowly repeated the grace, accenting each word referring to the Lord. When his father rose, the sign that the meal time was ended, Mary knew that the boy had pleased his father even though no praise was offered. Mary waited for her mother to rise, then followed her to the cooking area in the lean-to porch.

"Levi's eldest son came over today," Anna said. "Levi is very ill. I baked a honey cake for your father and me to take over this evening as soon as we are through straightening up from our meal. We won't be long."

"Let me go, too," Salome asked. "I can visit with Naomi. After all she is my best friend." The young girl's dark eyes pleaded.

Mary said, "I will do the straightening, Mother—so that you and Father may get to Levi's house before dark."

"That would be very nice, Mary, but are you sure you feel well enough?"

"Yes, I'm fine."

"May I go with you, Mother?" Salome begged. "Please?"

"No, Salome. You stay and help Mary watch over the boys. She's had a very wearing day."

"I'm fine," Mary cut in. "I'll tell the boys a story and put them to bed. Let her go. The girls won't make any noise to disturb Levi."

"We won't be gone long."

"Don't hurry!" *Oh no, do not hurry*, Mary pleaded inwardly, *I must find a way to talk to Joseph.*

She watched the three of them as they walked out into the golden sunset light. Her mother's red hair glistened in the fading glow of the sun, rich and coppery, worn in that same tight knot at the nape of her neck, no loose strands escaped their bonds after her mother had dressed them for the day. Mary noticed how Salome's shining black hair matched Joachim's. Mary thought, *The boys too have lustrous black hair. Images of their father with dark, deep-set eyes, broad friendly mouths, and firm set chins. They will be handsome young men in a few years. I am the only one who inherited the shining glow of our mother's hair and her flaxen-blue eyes.*

As soon as her parents turned the corner Mary let the boys join some neighborhood lads in a game of hide and seek. When she called them in they insisted on staying up until their parents returned, but Mary had other plans for her evening.

"Hurry, now. Get ready for bed and I'll tell you the story I promised."

"Tell the one about David and Goliath," David shouted.

"No. I want to hear one about Jonathan," the older boy, Jonathan Joachim, shouted louder. The argument heated. Mary ignored their pleas.

"I'm going to tell about Jonah and the whale." She began,
"This is the word of the Lord that came to
Jonah, son of Amittai . . . ." [4]

Long before the seamen cast Jonah into the sea the two boys had
fallen into the deep sleep of children who had run over hills, climbed
around rocks, and played games in gathering night shadows.

When she was certain that they would not call out for the
remainder of the story, Mary tiptoed into the living area and poured
fresh olive oil into the shallow lamp, lighted it from a glowing ember
of the oven, trimmed the wick, and set the flickering flame on the
table where it sent dots and dashes of lights over the walls. She
finger-combed her golden curls which persisted in poking wispy
tendrils from her headpiece. She pulled one of her mother's largest,
somber scarves about her and hurried into the darkening street which
led to Joseph's house.

Her heart beat rapidly since she knew that she should not be out
alone, but her need to share her news with Joseph outweighed her
fears of being caught. Levi and Josie lived in the opposite direction so
there was no chance of being seen by her parents but neighbors might
see her and tell her mother.

She walked where the shadows were deepest. The moon had not
yet risen but she knew it would be out soon, full and bright. She
rehearsed what she thought Joseph would say. She was certain that
the Lord would have told him because he would be expected to share
this birth, and the raising of the child, since he was her betrothed.
Joseph knew the Messiah was expected. He would be surprised, but
honored, that she had been chosen. He would understand her need for
care and affection.

When she reached his house she went to the door of his shop in
the cave behind his living quarters, stepped inside and timidly called
his name. Joseph rose from the lamplighted work table in the rear of
the cave and immediately took her arm and led her back to the street.

He looked to the right and to the left of the darkening narrow lane
and asked, "What are you doing here alone? It is not fitting for you
to be at my house with no companion."

"I need to talk with you," she said.

"It is not proper. I will come to your house."

"No. My parents are not home. I will go back. I apologize for coming." She knew that Joseph did not know her news. "Another time . . . ." she faltered. Not waiting for his reply she turned to run back down the lane toward her home. Now she knew that Gabriel had not spoken to either Joseph or her mother. She alone bore the impending future.

"Wait, Mary. I'll go back with you. It is too dark," Joseph called.

"No. No. I'm not afraid." She disappeared into the shadows. Panic overwhelmed her. Wondering what to do next, she raced over the rough cobbled street until she had reached the haven of her father's house. Not stopping to touch the mezuzah she fell onto the thin mat that was her bed and cried.

Through the narrow window Mary watched the moon rise to its fullness. Thin silver streaks sifted through clouds, making ladders of light, almost like the sun streaks she had seen shining though the clouds in the afternoon. A moon beam traced its way across the floor and touched her. A calmness soothed her. She knelt beside her pallet of reeds.

"*Boruch ato Adonai*," she began. "Blessed are You, O Lord our God, King of all the world, I am confused. I am proud to be your chosen hand-maiden yet I am afraid. I am so alone. I need to talk to someone . . . but who? You haven't sent Gabriel to tell my mother or Joseph, so you must not want them to share our secret. This is too much for me alone. I am afraid, My Lord, even though I should not be for I know you will protect Your Beloved Son. If no one knows and I have no proof that this child is Yours, I will be stoned to death just as Rebecca was. I can hear her screams now and I am sore afraid of the Law. You know the Law, Yahweh. You gave it to Moses." Tears ran down her cheeks. When she heard her parents' sandals scraping along the cobblestones she dried her face, lay on her bed pretending to be asleep.

As the steps stopped outside the door she heard her mother say, "I do declare the child is extremely upset, Joachim. Twice today she forgot the water jug and returned home looking pale. One time her dress was stained as if she had rolled in that red lily bed. This isn't like our Mary. Now if it were one of the boys coming home like that, saying that he had forgotten what he went after, I would understand as they are rattle-brained youngsters. But Mary—no. I think she's more upset about Rebecca's stoning than we realize."

"Good lesson for her—for all the young girls—not that our Mary would do such a thing. She's been brought up properly—to respect the Law—and Joseph is . . . ." As if he suddenly realized that Salome was standing with them, Joachim said, "It's time for you to go to bed, little girl."

It was but a moment until Salome pulled the drape to one side of the doorway and Mary felt her sister crawl on the pallet beside her own. Mary made no move to show that she was awake. Opening her eyes a slit she saw her parents kiss their fingers to the prayer box, as they slipped off their sandals, and tiptoed into the house. Mary had left the lamp lit and the flickering glow spattered light spots over their faces.

"Mary's so in love with Joseph," Anna said. "Young girls have such foolish dreams of love. I told her the other day how fortunate she was to know Joseph, that I hadn't laid eyes on you until our wedding ceremony."

"I remember that day, too." Joachim laughed. "I wondered how you would look when my father told me I was to marry little Anna, the young cousin of my brother's wife."

"When Elizabeth told me the betrothal had been made I hoped you'd be tall and handsome, like a prince. Ah, such dreams young girls have . . . ." Anna sighed and sat on a stool by the table.

"And what a let-down when you saw me, eh? Short and ugly as a toad—unfit to be a priest like my elder brother," Joachim said as he stood behind Anna. His broad shoulders were stooped from the years of bending over his work.

"I thought you were wonderful . . . and I still do. You have been such a patient husband and, as I told Mary, love really comes after marriage—with marriage, I should say."

"It's been a good life with you, Anna. The years have gone by too swiftly." He passed his work-gnarled hand over her russet hair.

Anna reached up and took his hand in hers, kissed it as she murmured, "You've worked so hard."

"So have you. We've worked together, with our Lord's help. We must know that our One Great Lord will look after us always."

Mary felt a tinge of guilt for eavesdropping. She was happy for them and wondered, *Will Joseph and I still be in love after we have been married many years?* She shivered. *What if Joseph will not accept my child? What if Mother and Father do not believe me? My condition will be noticeable within a few months.*

"God," she moved her lips as she prayed silently and fervently. "Help me. Please forgive me for being afraid. Hear my prayers for Rebecca, too. Surely you will forgive her for loving! Love is so—what would the world be without love? There would be no need for living! I thank you for Joseph—my dear Joseph. Without him I would not want to live. I pray that he will understand that I bear the Messiah. Yahweh, I trust you to take care of me . . . but right now I need someone to talk to."

She recalled Gabriel's message about Elizabeth. If an old woman could be with child, truly that would be a sign. She thought that she would have to see for herself by going to Elizabeth's. But Elizabeth and her husband, Zechariah, lived near Jerusalem, a three or four day trip by caravan from Nazareth.

"Oh, Dear Lord, our One God, lead me . . . ." Mary fell asleep without finishing the prayer.

Chapter Five

Rebecca s Final Rites

Sun rays crept over Mary's bed. Fragrant smoke curls twisted into the narrow windows along with the sounds of her parents' morning rituals: her mother building a fire in the courtyard oven while her father was chanting morning prayers. Even after the night's sleep Mary was tired. She had dreamed the same dream, over and over. All night she had been terrorized by a mob stoning her while she called out for help. No one seemed to hear her cries or to come to save her from the bruising rain of rocks.

Quietly she pulled herself off the pallet, rolled it and place it in the corner. She donned a fresh blue robe, tied a thin braided belt about her slim waist as she whispered,

"Blessed are you, O Lord our God, King of all the
world, who gives clothes to cover our bodies." [1]

When she went to splash cool water on her face her mother said, "Daughter Mary, you look weary this morning. Didn't you sleep well."

"I was restless. I kept dreaming that I was Rebecca."

Joachim concluded his prayers. As he sat cross-legged at the low table he said, "My Daughter, you must not make yourself ill over Rebecca's mistakes." Immediately he began to eat from the bowl of steaming lentil pulse Anna had placed before her husband. Neither Anna nor Mary spoke as he repeatedly pulled a piece of golden crust from a round loaf in the center of the table, curving the edges of the crust into a spoon to scoop some of the hot porridge from the bowl to his mouth. He finished his breakfast with soft bread dipped into a bowl of honey. Then, after licking the sweetness from his lips and the hairs about his mouth, he said his private grace, and went into his workshop.

Mary remained at the table and toyed with a piece of crust, edged with honey, then left it in her bowl uneaten. She left the table and picked up a scarf which she had doffed the evening before and tied it about her head.

"I'll be back before long, Mother," she said.

"Going to the well so early?" Anna asked.

"No, I am going to see Rebecca's mother."

"Do you think that is wise? The disgrace and all."

"Surely, Mother, you would not have me be as unfeeling as an infidel. *Adonai* is a forgiving God. He does not carry a grudge against Rebecca or her family. She has paid for any error in judgement that she made," Mary said as she walked across the room. Leaning against the doorway she touched the prayer box. *"Adonai,"* she whispered, *"Help me. Tell me what to do. Please give me the strength to do what is right."*

"What did you say, Mary?", her mother asked.

"I asked our Lord to guide me, Mother. I must go to Rebecca's mother."

"Mary, you cannot go alone. I will go with you," Anna stepped to the shop door and called, raising her voice to compete with the noise of a wooden mallet striking wood.

"Joachim," she called. "Mary and I are going to see Rebecca's mother."

"Indeed, you will not," he shouted. His angry voice startled both Anna and Mary. They stepped back as he rushed through the door. "I will not have my family's honor soiled by associating with . . . ."

In a low voice, a startling contrast to her father's shouts, Mary finished his sentence, ". . . a grieving mother? You have taught me that *Adonai* is a forgiving God. Surely we, too, can forgive."

She walked out into the early dawn. Anna threw a scarf about her head and joined her daughter as Joachim strode out of the house with authority in every step. He called out loudly,

"Mary! Anna! I forbid you to go! Come back here!"

Ignoring his shouts mother and daughter walked on toward the Road of Merchants. The sun brightened the sky with rose and gold, dissolving the night mist. Nazareth was not yet fully awake. Here and there farmers and traders with produce lashed on the backs of asses and camels lumbered along the narrow street toward the city market.

Mary and her mother came to the white wall surrounding Nathan's silent house. There were no sounds of sorrow. The professional mourners, customary at every home with a deceased family member, were not wailing inside or outside the wall. Mary pushed aside the wrought iron gate in the wall and followed the path of smooth stepping stones up to the ornate door at the front of the two-story white stone house. No one answered Anna's knocking or her repeated calls, "Any one here?"

"This is strange," Anna said.

The door was ajar and they looked in. A chilling silence hung over the ornately furnished room with its bright Persian rugs and imported Roman furniture. In the center of the room lay the broken, beaten body of Rebecca. Both father and mother seemed to be stunned, paralyzed by the return and the dumping of the body. There was no way of knowing how long Rebecca's remains had been lying there in the silent room.

Still and unseeing as a statue dressed in a pale green silken gown, Rebecca's mother was seated on the floor staring at the bruised and bloodied body of her daughter lying on a lustrous rug. Across the room Nathan sat beside an open door, facing the formal courtyard. He wore the same black silk robe Mary had ripped while trying to stop his throwing stones with the others.

Mary shuddered. The horror of yesterday morning came flooding back. All the terror she had experienced returned at the sight of Rebecca's battered, broken body. She leaned against the door and closed her eyes trying to stop the tears, but the tears flowed into rivulets on her cheeks. Anna moved forward into the entry room holding Mary's hand tightly clasped in her own.

Mary pulled away from her mother and kneeled beside Rebecca's grieving mother. The woman looked up and held her arms out to embrace her visitor.

"Mary," she whispered and broke into wailing with great heavy sobs. "Mary, look what they have done with my beautiful baby, my beautiful Rebecca." The calling of her name brought on a spasm of grief and tears. Mary could find no voice to answer.

Anna had already assessed the needs of the moment. She leaned down and whispered to Mary, "Come out into the hall. We must talk." She walked to the doorway and Mary followed. Not wanting to break the silence of the house Anna continued whispering. "It is past dawn yet the body has not been prepared for burial. Where are their friends who should have cleansed the girl and wrapped her in her shroud?"

"Perhaps everyone is afraid to touch her, believing she is defiled and that touching her would defile themselves."

"Does her sin excuse the sin of omission of honoring the dead before Our Lord?" Anna asked while removing her shawl. "I shall prepare her myself. Get water and cloths for me. You will have to go back to our house to get the white linen winding sheet which I have put aside for a member of our family when it is needed. I'm sure this family has one ready but it would be useless to ask either of them where we could find it.

"Tell your father to make a funeral board and to bring men with him to accompany the body to the burying cave."

"Do you think Father . . . ?"

"He will put up an argument but don't take 'no' for an answer," Anna replied with the voice of authority, then shaking her head and gesturing with outstretched hands she went on, "You will have no problem, Mary. You know he'll do anything to please you." She paused and then, as an after thought, added, "Arouse Salome and have her see that the boys are dressed properly and fed. They may want to come with their father. Then, go ask the rabbi to come here. He will understand the need. These parents are so grief stricken they are like the dead themselves. They need help."

As if to bolster Anne's statement of the urgent need Rebecca's mother broke her silent vigil to grieve aloud. The father began to mourn, crying loud and with deep wails he knelt beside his dead daughter, begging her forgiveness. As he ripped his heavy silk robe into shreds, poured ashes upon his head, and tore out wads of his graying hair, he babbled as a madman, seeking comfort from his daughter's corpse.

Mary was torn by her conflicting emotions. *I feel sorry for him,* she thought, *but he brought this on himself. Greedy, that's what he was. How can I feel bitterness toward the man when I feel sorrow, too? He is a tormented man who will never again know peace of mind. How could he have let himself be so angry that he would not only condone but also aid the stoning of his only daughter? How could any man do that?*

Of course, everyone will blame Rebecca. She should not have broken the Law. She did not talk to me about Laban. I did not realize what she was doing when she told me how much she hated thinking of being married to Benjamin. She was wrong, but she was trying to escape thinking about spending the rest of her life with someone she abhorred. Poor Rebecca. She did not escape. Though maybe she is happy now. I hope so.

Anna knelt and began removing Rebecca's tattered garments. Mary found tepid water beside the empty baking oven and brought several basins full. She found towels hanging on the bushes still slightly damp from the night air.

"Go now," Anna said. "Go and bring the linen. You will find a vial of myrrh with the sheet. Bring that, too. I shall anoint her in the Lord's name if there is no one else to do it."

Mary ran and arriving home, breathing heavily, rushed into the shop where her father was drilling a hole in a piece of wood. Joachim listened with his head turned from her as she relayed her mother's message. She ended her request with, "I'm sure Joseph will come along if you ask him."

"We should not interfere," Joachim said.

"Interfere? Father, a girl . . . only fourteen years old, the same age as I, lies battered by rocks. She was my friend. Would you deny her a decent burial? What kind of man are you? Have you no heart?"

"I will have to search how the Law reads about honoring a mortal sinner."

"If she sinned a mortal sin her mortal body paid the highest price. Please, don't make her soul pay into eternity!"

"What do you know about a soul . . . about eternity?"

"I know nothing, Father, except that if our *Adonai* is a good God, as you have taught me, I think he gave people souls to live on after death. I don't know how or where . . . but Father . . . even if I'm wrong, what's the harm in helping a mother through a nightmare? Think how it would be if I were dead instead of Rebecca. Wouldn't you hope that someone would care?"

"I thank *Adonai,* Mary, that you are so pure and full of His perfection your mother and I would never have to live through such an ordeal."

"Then repay *Adonai* now, for you never know what you might have to meet some day," she said and thought as tears welled in her eyes, *You might have to face this same ordeal if no one believes me. Adonai, forgive me for doubting but I am afraid. I am sore afraid.*

Seeing her tears Joachim turned, laid aside his drill, then came to her and enfolded her in his arms. "Don't cry, my little Daughter. I do thank Our God for you every day. I will do as you ask. If I cannot find enough men I shall bring a cart."

Mary kissed her father's cheek and went in to arouse the rest of the family. Salome, delighted to be considered adult enough to be responsible for her brothers, assumed her tasks of preparing breakfast plus overseeing the boys' dressing and the rolling up of their pallets.

Mary found the neatly folded length of white linen, wrapped and sewn in heavy cotton cloth to keep it clean for it important future use. In the same package was the myrrh. Holding the bundle against her chest, she ran to the synagogue.

"You must come, Rabbi," she panted. "You are needed."

"But the girl, Rebecca, broke the sacred Law. The Law must be honored, Mary. I cannot . . . ."

Mary broke into his sentence, "What I am asking you to do does not break the Law. You are needed by Nathan and his wife. They are in shock. Remember, Rabbi, Nathan is a generous supporter of this synagogue. How better could you serve your congregation than by earning Nathan's undying gratitude for your help in his time of need? I tell you these parents are so stricken they are like the dead themselves."

"I will go with you, Mary. You plead like a lawyer before King David's royal court. But I will not touch that defiled body."

"No need for that. My mother and I . . . ."

"You say Anna is in on this also? And your father? What is Joachim's position?"

Mary was already several paces ahead of the old man and did not answer his question. *Let him find out when he gets there,* she thought.

I wonder if Father will find enough men. Yes, he will. Father is very persuasive when he wants to be.

While Mary was gone Anna labored over Rebecca's battered body. Preparing the dead was not new to her but she had always been a part of a team of women performing the required sacred duties. She washed the blood and clay from Rebecca's long black hair and fanned it out to hasten its drying. She worried that she was not as gentle with the body as she would like to be, especially when she turned the now stiffened corpse.

The bereaved mother and father had not stirred. If they saw Anna working over their daughter's body they had looked through dazed eyes that did not register any activity.

With all her errands finished Mary returned to the house of sorrow with the rabbi following closely. Anna looked up, saw Mary and said, "I'm so glad to have you back. I need your help." Together they wound the seemingly endless white linen cloth about the slender corpse. Even as the two women struggled with the unwieldy body the rabbi did not offer to help. The three of them understood that the Law forbade him to touch a dead body.

"Mary, see if you can find two coins," Anna said. "I have tried to close Rebecca's eyelids but they will not remain shut."

Mary searched and found two gold aurei in a shallow dish on a shelf. She looked away while her mother pressed the two coins over her friend's eyelids.

After standing at the door for a while the rabbi walked slowly toward the statue-like mother. He gently touched her shoulder and the woman suddenly shouted,

"He killed her. He killed my baby!" She pointed toward the lone figure silhouetted against the rising sun. "He killed her," she screamed and picking up a heavy copper urn she rushed toward her husband. The astonished rabbi ran behind her, pulled at her upraised arms to stop her. She fought with the small, bent old man who had come to bless her. Fought like a wild, attacking tiger.

Mary ran to help the old man.

"Please," she begged as she held the distraught woman's arms, "there has been enough violence. Do not blacken Rebecca's memory more."

The hysterical woman sank onto a satin covered couch. "My Rebecca . . . ," she cried. "My beautiful Rebecca."

"Let her cry," the rabbi said. "That will help her more than any words we can say."

After his wife's attack Nathan remained crouched beside the door leading to the garden. Nathan began to mourn slowly, crying aloud with deep wails as he crawled over to his dead daughter's wrapped body and begged her forgiveness.

Mary was surprised how quickly her own father had been able to round up the band of men gathered outside the door of the merchant's house. When she saw Joseph among the somber-robed men the horror of the past minutes were erased. She felt an overwhelming love for her husband-to-be, handsome and tall, his trim black beard and hair glistening in the sunshine, a head above the nine men, now ten, as the old rabbi joined them. Their exchanged glance was brief but his dark eyes returned her love for him. It was obvious that he adored her.

"Where are the children?" Mary asked her father.

"Salome is keeping them at home. I thought the day would be too difficult for the young boys," Joachim said.

Mary nodded in agreement and turned to watch her mother organize the funeral. Anna supervised the placing of the body on the carrying board and the balancing of the girl's weight on the men's shoulders. Joseph was taller than the others so she put him at the rear of the bearers where he held the board with his hands. In spite of the rabbi's pleading the merchant father remained at the house, raving through the empty rooms, screaming in a shrill voice, pleading with the Lord to help him.

The procession to the caves was small. Rebecca's weeping mother, supported between Anna and Mary, followed the black-robed rabbi and the men bearing the white wrapped figure on a plank. No one had arranged to hire professional mourners. The funeral walk was silent.

The slow-moving group was almost at the edge of town when Nathan, his tattered robe flapping in the wind of his swift steps, hurried to join them. No longer screaming, but weeping with great sobs, he clutched at his wife's robe, then grasping her hand he begged for her forgiveness. As the two clung to each other Mary and her mother stepped aside and continued the slow walk, plodding on with an even steadiness until they reached the caves of the dead.

Mary watched as Rebecca's body was carried into the dark cavern. With the two mothers she stopped and stood at the narrow opening. Faint lights flickering from burning torches and the low rumble of male voices chanting prayers filtered out to them. After securing Rebecca's body in the cave and sealing it with rocks, the men paused to chat. Then with lighter steps they made their ways back to Nazareth.

The rabbi walked between Nathan and his wife. Joachim joined Anna and Joseph left the group of men to walk beside Mary.

"Mary, I'm sorry I spoke so abruptly to you last night," he said quietly.

"But you were right. I shouldn't have come to your house alone," she whispered.

"What did you need?"

"Nothing, really."

"I know that isn't true. You would not have come if you didn't have a good reason."

"Well, I just wondered if you had heard anything about the Messiah?"

"Only that one is expected," he answered. With a quizzical expression he looked down at her and asked, "Why do you want to know?"

"I just wondered if He is expected soon."

"So some believe. But it my understanding that first Elijah is to return and prepare the way for the one who is to be borne by a virgin."

"A royal virgin, I assume?"

"Of course. How could we expect to get a great leader who will free us from the heel of the Romans if he does not come from royal stock with exceptional breeding, education . . . and great wealth?"

"One would feel that is so," Mary said. She stepped on a loose rock, her step faltered and Joseph steadied her.

"Be careful, Mary," her mother called. "Remember how you fell yesterday. You know, it could be the heat making you unsteady."

"I'm fine, Mother. I just slipped on those rolling pebbles. Luckily Joseph caught me."

"It's always nice to have a strong man around," her mother smiled at Joachim. Her parents slowed their steps and fell in beside Mary and Joseph. A pall of silence fell over the walkers. Mary stared straight ahead, thinking.

Gabriel has not told Mother or Joseph. Both believe that the chosen virgin will be one of royalty. If no one believes me that I am the chosen virgin my family may be walking this same path in a few months leaving my body in a cave near Rebecca's. She shuddered and closed her eyes, holding tighter to Joseph's arm for support.

"I hope we didn't interrupt a private conversation," Anna said.

"Oh, no," Joseph spoke up quickly. "We were just discussing the coming of a Messiah."

"Lots of talk about that," Joachim said. "The need for a leader is in the hearts of all freedom loving men."

"Odd you two should be talking about the Messiah today," Anna turned to face Mary. "Just yesterday you asked me that, didn't you?'

"Not surprising at all, Anna. This subject is discussed everywhere these days," Joachim said.

When they reached their garden gate, Mary loosened her hold on Joseph's arm and said, "Excuse me, Joseph, but it is late for me to be going to the well."

"Salome could go for you," Anna said.

"No, Mother, it is my duty." She turned again toward Joseph and said, "You understand? I must go to the well."

He reached for her arm and pulled her closer to him and whispered, "No, I don't understand. You wanted to talk to me and you won't tell me why."

"Forget it, Joseph. I found out what I needed to know. Now, I must go to the well." Mary darted toward the door and ran into the house. Joseph was gone when she came out with two pitchers.

I'm glad he's gone. I feel the need to be close to Adonai. Perhaps he will speak to me while I'm at the well and will tell me what to do. My mind is in a whirl. One day! Only one day changed my world. Was it only yesterday?"

As she ran along the footpath she replayed all the drama she had been a part of. As she went to the well a white dove fluttered from its perch in the rocks and darted in and out from rock to bush to a low limb of the willow tree. Mary called to it, cooing a soft imitation of its own song. While she was still unsure of what was taking place with her life, Mary walked home with a soothed spirit.

Chapter Six

Does Elizabeth Know the Answer?

Mary dressed, smoothed her hair under her kerchief then knelt for her morning devotions, but her mind kept drifting from her prayer to Elizabeth. *Elizabeth must have the answer to the puzzle since Gabriel mentioned her name. Why else would he tell me about her? But how could I ever get to her house? The three or four day walk between Nazareth and Jerusalem might as well be three hundred days. I couldn't walk that far through desert and mountains all alone.*

How could I convince my parents that I need to go to Elizabeth's house? I know they would consider such a long journey a most unusual request.

She practiced several starts of a conversation, mouthing them silently, not wanting to awaken her sister who was lying on her mat nearby.

"Father and Mother, I want to go visit dear cousin Elizabeth."

"Why?" they would ask.

"No," she whispered. "I should start out with, 'Dear Mother and Father, I am longing to visit Cousin Elizabeth.'

"'When did such a longing come over you? You've never wanted to go there before.' they would say.

"*Boruch ato Adonai.* Blessed are you, O Lord Our God. Guide my tongue to speak the right words."

When Mary stepped into the kitchen her father had finished a bowl of hot pulse and had a piece of warm bread dripping with golden honey in his hand. He did not pause in his eating as Mary sat beside him. Her mother, who was out in the courtyard stoking the morning fire to bread-baking heat, came in saying,

"Mary, I heard you crying in the night. Were you dreaming again?"

"Yes, Mother. I'm sorry if I awakened you."

"You must not take Rebecca's fate so hard. It wasn't your fault and you don't have to shoulder her sins."

"But, Mother . . ."

"We all know how difficult it is . . your experiencing a friend's death would naturally be upsetting. Your father and I talked about it last night and we are worried about you."

"Do not worry about me, I shall keep busy and hope one day to stop reliving this nightmare."

"Pray to the Lord, our One God," her father said.

"Yes, my Father, I shall pray. With *Adonai's* help I will find my way."

The Sabbath passed and it was almost time for another when Mary quietly stepped through the front door of her home as the sun streaked the dawn sky with red. She drew a shawl about her for warmth against the chilled air.

"Mary," her mother called. The young girl stopped and turned. "Mary, where are you going so early?"

"To the synagogue, my Mother."

"Why Mary?"

"To pray to *Adonai*," she bowed her head as she said the holy word.

"You can pray to the Lord in our home, Mary. You do not need to go to the synagogue for that. He is not there. He is in the great temple at Jerusalem."

"I know that *Adonai* is everywhere, my Mother. Everywhere. But I feel close to him at the synagogue where the Torah is enshrined."

"You have been slipping out at dawn for days now, not telling us where you were going. Why, Mary?"

"I told you. I go to talk with *Adonai*."

"You've been doing this ever since the day Rebecca was stoned. Does that incident have anything to do with your secretive actions?"

"I suppose so. That day brought many problems to my mind. I'm trying to solve them."

"Go to the rabbi. He is a wise teacher."

"He did not aid Rebecca in her search for answers," Mary lowered her head as she answered softly.

"But surely you do not have a great problem like Rebecca's. Or do you, Mary? You have not been unfaithful to your betrothed?"

"Unfaithful to Joseph? Oh no, Mother, I love him very much."

"Josie told me yesterday that you have been going to see Rebecca's mother each day."

"Yes, Mother, I have. When I get the water for our house I stop by and get her jug so that she doesn't have to go to the spring. Rebecca was her only daughter, you know."

"They have servants for that task."

"True. But her mother needs someone to talk to. All their friends have deserted them as though they, too, were guilty of a crime. How can that be—a crime of love causing so much sorrow?"

"Passion, my daughter, not love. Love would not expose a young girl to such an ending. Passion, yes. It was a crime, Mary. A crime against the betrothed husband. How can you stand up for that girl?"

"Because she was my friend. She was not evil, Mother. Rebecca was a victim of men. Women have no rights in this world. It is not fair."

"Fair or not, a woman receives the respect she earns!"

"Oh, Mother, you are so old fashioned. You still believe it is right for a man to own a wife like a chattel." Mary stepped from the doorway and said, "Someday—someday women and men will be equal. A woman will be looked upon as an equal partner, not a possession. I may not ever see the time but it will happen, Mother. It will happen!"

"Come back into the house, Mary. The chill is great out here." She put her arms about the girl and shepherded her back to the table where Joachim was finishing his breakfast. "Your father and I have been talking and we think you have let this Rebecca incident bother you too much."

"Incident? Death by stoning! You call that an incident? It is barbaric—not befitting *Adonai's* people."

"Whatever—it is the Law," Anna said.

"I cannot believe that our Lord gave us that law—I still believe it was created by men, for men. You'll never convince me that a loving God would be so cruel," Mary shook her head slowly.

"Your father and I think perhaps you might need to get away from here for a while. How would you like to go visit our cousin Elizabeth?"

Mary looked up quickly, not quite believing what she had heard.

Anna went on, "She has asked for you to come so many times, and now that you are going to be married soon, you would not be able to visit her later. Last evening your father talked with friends of Levi who are going to Jerusalem in a few days. They are joining a caravan from Damascus and will be happy to have you ride with them. You could help care for the children."

Before she answered, Mary lowered her eyes, locked her hands in a prayerful manner and silently gave thanks to her Lord. Slowly she raised her head and said, "I think I would like to visit Cousin Elizabeth very much. As I remember she has a lovely house on a hill where many flowers grow. It should be very beautiful this time of year. But how would I go? What will I ride? We have no ass, no camel."

Her father paused in his eating. "You will ride with the children. They will bring an extra ass."

"And how shall I return?"

"The family will be returning in two or three months. The man, Ishmael, has business in Jerusalem, a short distance from Ein Karen where Elizabeth lives. His wife is taking the children there to visit with her parents. The weather will be cool and should be quite pleasant."

"I shall miss you," Mary said, knowing her parents would expect her to express regret to be leaving them.

"We will miss you too, Mary, but we both think it will be a nice change for you. You may take some of your embroidery along. Cousin Elizabeth is a fine artisan with the needle and she can teach you many things useful in a home. She taught me so very much."

"I always thought that she was your aunt. She's so much older than you."

"No, she is the eldest daughter of my Aunt Sophia who raised me after my parents died. Her husband, the priest Zechariah, is the one who helped make the arrangements with your father's father for our marriage. They were both priests at the temple in Jerusalem."

"Father, since you are of the division of Abijah why didn't you become a priest?" Mary asked.

"I studied for the priesthood for a period of time but I didn't like it. I enjoyed working with my hands more. Wood felt better than books. Besides I didn't look like a priest should. Everyone, even my brothers, told me I was too ugly, bandy-legged and broad."

"As if looks make a difference to the Lord," Mary said, kissing him on his forehead. "I shall be honored to go to Cousin Elizabeth's. I must tell Joseph. I hope he will understand."

"It is not fitting for you to go to his house. I'll stop by and tell him to come over today and you can tell him then," her father said.

"Have him come over for the evening meal, Joachim," Anna said, "and bring his father too. They probably get tired of their own cooking."

She poured water into a basin, washed her hands and began her daily task of bread-making. She added handfuls of flour to the bowl of the bubbling starter dough she had put aside from yesterday's baking, then adding oil and water, she kneaded and slapped the soft mound before she covered it with a white linen cloth.

Mary picked up the water jug and walked down the road toward the spring. As she walked up the graveled path she saw the lilies and smiled as she thought of the secret between the Most High and herself. *God does move in mysterious ways.*

Chapter Seven

Joseph's Gift to Mary

While her mother prepared the evening meal, Mary was anxious to get to the well and back quickly since Joseph and his father were to be special guests. She hurried to the graveled path and met three girls returning from the well. She realized that she had not seen her friends since the morning they had come running to tell her about Rebecca's stoning. Ever since that fateful morning she had not visited the well at a regular time as she did when she and Rebecca walked the path together. Often she was late since she spent much time with Rebecca's mother. Her days had been so filled with worry she hadn't even missed their playful girl-talk chatter. The thought crossed her mind that perhaps they had been avoiding her because she had rudely left them at the bluff. Then she wondered if their parents had not approved of Rebecca's funeral. She shrugged. It made no difference. The Lord's work had to be done even if some people didn't approve.

"We haven't seen you, Mary. Where have you been?"

Mary smiled, "Busy helping my mother."

"We hear you've been spending time with Nathan's wife. Too bad about Rebecca. But she should have known better than to cheat on Benjamin," one of the girls said and another added, "I don't blame her for cheating on that old man, but don't tell my folks I said that."

Mary spoke up quickly, "Rebecca paid too high a price. It was wrong. Men have no right to stone a woman no matter what she's done." Mary went on toward the well leaving the three girls standing in the path, surprised at her words.

Mary filled her pitcher and started back down the hill when a sudden chill came over her. *What if Joseph will not want me? What if he doubts that I am carrying the Messiah? What if he thinks I have been untrue to him?* Her steps slowed as she made her way down the worn, stone path edging the outcropping of rock. She stopped beside the blood red lilies and their fragrance enveloped her.

A mantle of calm spread over her. *Our Lord created and continues to care for these flowers by sending rain and sunshine to make them grow, she thought. I know He will keep watch over me and His Child for I have been chosen by Him.* As she continued down the path she recalled the lines from one of Solomon's Songs,

"My beloved is mine and I am his, his pasture; his flock among the lilies." [1]

She chanted the words over and over reinforcing her courage as she walked down the deserted hillside.

At home she saw her two brothers outside the gate. They did not see her as they were looking the other way, seemingly watching something. She came up behind them and asked, "What are you doing?"

Both turned and answered at once, "We're waiting for Joseph and his father. We are to run in and tell Mother that the guests are nearing."

Mary laughed. *Oh it is indeed a joyous day*, she thought as she went into the house and found the household bustling with preparations for the special occasion. Joachim had bought lamb to serve. That alone was a signal something unusual was about to happen. Salome had gathered green leeks to add to the stew made with dried lentils which Anna kept stored in round earthenware pots. The savory aroma of simmering meat and spices filled the house.

Mary cut fresh cucumber slices for a cool, crunchy contrast to the hot, somewhat greasy stew. She arranged the thin green circles on a tray then fussed about straightening the room, rearranging flowers she had put on the table earlier that afternoon. This was to be a special night for her. She wondered, *How will Joseph take my going away before our wedding. Should I tell him why I need to be with Elizabeth? No*, she decided. *Now is not the proper time.*

The sun was slipping down behind the distant hills when the two guests arrived. Mary had her usual heart-pounding reaction at the sight of her betrothed. She stood inside the door listening while her father went out to greet the guests. Mary spread the draperies closing off her sleeping area to peek out. She watched her father pour wine into three glasses. Toasts of deep friendship were exchanged between the two fathers and extended to the younger man. Joseph stood almost a head taller than the fathers. And of course, he was more handsome. He glanced here and there, nodding his head in agreement now and then with whatever the older men were saying.

Mary smiled. She knew he was hoping to see her, but good manners required that she remain out of sight until her father called for her. First he would call for his wife Anna to come greet their honored guests. At last the moment arrived. Mary answered immediately as she heard her name spoken.

She bowed to her own father, then she acknowledge the feeble, shaking Jacob, and moved toward Joseph. Again she lowered her head, demurely looking to the side to avoid direct eye contact. He took her hand in his and she felt blood rushing over her whole body. She hated blushing, the exposing of her inner feelings. She looked up hesitantly. He smiled. Then she didn't care that she had blushed. There was no need denying that she loved him.

Dinner went well. The three men ate ravenously. Anna was pleased. "When men eat, I know I've cooked the dinner right," she would always say. After the men had finished and retired outside to walk and relieve themselves of the pangs of overeating, Anna and the children sat down to enjoy the feast. Mary toyed with the food. She was so excited about her trip. Nothing had been said during the meal. She wondered when the proper time would come to announce her journey. With the serving of the sweet cakes Joachim said,

"Our Mary has something to share with us."

"You tell them , Father."

"Very well, if you so wish, my Daughter. Mary's mother and I think Mary should go to Ein Karen to visit with her cousin Elizabeth before the wedding. We think she needs to get away from Nazareth for a while. She has been overwrought about the stoning – being the first she ever saw it has upset her."

Salome and the two boys clamored, "We want to go too. Why should Mary go and leave us home? Please," they all joined in the chorus.

"No, I'm afraid you can't go along this time. You see Father found a job for me. I am to help care for several children of a family going to Ein Karen by caravan. Next week. Isn't this exciting? My very first trip without my parents," she laughed.

Joseph said, "This is what you wanted to tell me, Mary, and you were afraid?"

"Of you, Joseph? Why would I be afraid to tell you?"

"You've acted rather mysteriously and I've wondered if I had cut you off too quickly."

She looked directly into his eyes with her own wide open. Please don't mention that I was at your house, they pleaded. She willed her message to be understood.

"I think it is a splendid idea," he nodded to Joachim and Anne. "Mary has been under a great strain. I have known that ever since that terrible day."

Relieved that her secret was safe, she smiled at Salome and her brothers. "We have a few days before I leave. We'll plan something very special. Be thinking about what we could do."

Several days after the dinner party evening shadows were beginning to stretch from house to house when Mary saw Joseph coming down the narrow lane. She went to the door and turned to her mother and said,

"Joseph is coming this way leading a little ass." She ran to meet him and grasped the red tooled-leather harness as she nuzzled her head against the little shoulder-high animal, whose gray coat glistened with a recent brushing.

"What a dear animal," she said. With gentle strokes she caressed the long ears as they moved back and forth.

"She is for you, my Betrothed Wife. A pre-wedding gift. I wanted to be sure you had a sturdy and gentle beast to ride on your journey."

"But, Joseph, there is no need."

"The men at the stable made jokes when I told them I was buying the animal for you. 'Yaha,' they laughed. 'Your bride-to-be is going away from you now? So soon before the wedding? What will she do after you are wed?' I told them it was not their affair to worry about." He smiled and touched her arm. "It is good that you will be visiting your cousin, although I shall miss you, Mary."

Mary looked up and brushed his cheek with her hand. "You are a dear one, Joseph, and I shall treasure this gift. Does she have a name?"

"Yes. Jericho."

"Jericho. I like that. Come along, Jericho," she said as they walked toward the walled courtyard at the back of the house. "We'll find a nice place to tether you for the night."

"I brought her over early so you'd have several days to get acquainted and become friends," Joseph said.

"I f eel that we are good friends now. I love her, Joseph, and now I'm more excited than ever about the trip. My very own animal on my very first journey alone. Well, not really alone. I'll be riding with a family in the caravan. But I feel grown-up, at last." She looked up at Joseph and her eyes grew wide as she said, "I hope I won't be afraid or get homesick."

"You'll do fine, Mary. *Adonai* will be with you, so have no fear. The caravan should be very interesting with people from many countries. You'll see merchants from Damascus with silks and rugs, perfumes, dates, grain, and every other tradable item."

"Yes, I know," Mary said with feigned enthusiasm. She wasn't as joyous as she was pretending to be. She did not want to leave Joseph, but she felt driven by the need to talk to Elizabeth. Surely *Adonai* had planned it so.

Chapter Eight

Mary Leaves Her Family

The week went by swiftly. Salome took over the duty of going to the well for water. Mary and her mother were busy packing things she would need for the trip: clothing, a bedroll, heavy shawl, and food. The boys didn't go outside to play as much as the two women would have liked. They seemed to be in the way all the time, tailing Mary as she worked at every task. The arrival of Jericho solved that problem. The boys spent every day riding and grooming the new family pet.

Mary was folding her clothing into a bag made of heavy dark sailcloth, tied with a heavy fisherman's net rope while her mother filled a basket with food.

"I've packed several honey cakes and loaves of bread plus a package of dates, nuts and fruits you may share with the family you will be riding with," Anna said then she added in a wistful voice, "I wish I were going with you, Mary. I would love to see my dear cousin. I feel so sorry for her in spite of her wealth. Poor dear, barren all these years. What a heartache that has been to her and to her husband, Zechariah. I'm sure they feel a certain amount of shame that our Lord did not see fit to bless them with children. Now both of them are long past their primes and they have no hopes of ever having a son to carry on the priestly tradition of the family."

"But they have each other, Mother. They are such loving people." Mary longed to tell her mother the exciting news that soon Elizabeth would be having that son but she felt honor bound to keep Gabriel's secret until she had talked to her cousin.

"Elizabeth and Zechariah are devoted to our *Adonai*. I do believe their every moment is filled with devotions to Him."

"I haven't been with them much, but I remember that Elizabeth was like a warm grandmother. Since I never knew your mother, I always think of her that way. She is a lot older than you, isn't she?

"She must be about sixty now. I don't keep track of my own years—let alone hers. But we both have a few gray hairs to tell the tale."

"Very few, Mother, if any. Right now I cannot see a single one. But Cousin Elizabeth's hair was very gray when we visited her years ago. I think that was why I thought she was old. I'm really looking forward to visiting her. It is wonderful of you and Father to be so thoughtful of me."

"My dear, there's nothing your father and I wouldn't do for you that we could. Do try to rid yourself of your grief over Rebecca while you are gone."

"Yes, Mother I will try. I will pray everyday for guidance."

On the morning of the day that Mary was to start her journey her family went to the crossroad with her. Joseph joined them and carried the bundle of her clothing while Mary sat primly on a bright blanket atop Jericho, testing out her skills at maneuvering the little beast by pulling on the narrow braided reins.

"You're very good at riding, my Daughter. Now doesn't she look like a seasoned traveler atop that ass?"

Joachim patted the two young boys on the shoulder. Both David and Jonathan were sad that the day had came for Mary to leave . . . not only would they miss their favorite sister but now she was taking away their favorite amusement of riding Jericho.

Salome pouted and cried all that morning hoping her tears would change her parents' minds. Mary promised to bring a gift from Jerusalem for her. The promise of a silk scarf of many colors quieted her briefly. Later Mary reminded her sister that she would have the whole room to herself, small as it was. But that did not convince the younger girl that her parents were right in letting her older sister go alone.

Anna and Joseph stood on either side of Mary, who remained mounted on Jericho, and did not enter into the chatter that went between the girl and the children. Mary was so busy trying to make them happy about her leaving that she didn't notice the caravan approaching in the distance. Joachim had seen it and had walked to meet the leading group of men riding on asses.

Joachim and Ishmael, who lived north of Nazareth, exchanged greetings. There was a carnival air about the meeting of the two families. The caravan of plodding camels, loaded and swaying from side to side, kept on their slow forward march as the traveling companions introduced themselves: Ishmael, his wife Rachel, and their three small boys who were four, six, and eight years old.

Mary took the youngest, David, to ride with her. The other boys rode asses on either side of her. The mother's mount was similar in size and color to Jericho except that its harness was decorated with many bright red and yellow yarn tassels. Ishmael, the father, rode a large, almost black, animal and leading a mare loaded with personal baggage. He fastened Mary's things on the extra ass which he had brought along for her to ride. By the time Mary and her new family were ready to leave, the caravan had lumbered on, making a heavy dust cloud for them to follow.

Smiling, Anna and Joseph clutched Mary's hands and wished her well on her journey. Salome and the boys broke into tears. Joachim lifted the smaller boy in his arms and led the children away.

"God be with you!" Anna and Joseph called. Mary's eyes were misty and her chin quivered as she called her last goodbyes to them.

"Boruch ato Adonai" she whispered. *"Help me to be brave so that my family will not worry about me."*

"Why are you crying, Mary?" the four year old asked. "Are you sorry you are going with us?"

"No, of course not," Mary smiled and held him close to her. "I always cry when I leave my loved ones.

"Will you cry when you leave me?"

"Of course I will!" she said.

Mary's new family caught up with the other riders following the burdened camels. Over hundreds of years, a constant stream of caravans had beaten a hard road beneath a thick layer of dust. A steady breeze stirred loosened dust into a thick, gritty cloud. Mary pulled her scarf tighter to cover her nose, and looped the ends of the boys' turbans to protect their faces.

Mary was not accustomed to keeping her balance on the back of an animal. She kept her eyes averted from the laden beasts ahead as their constant swaying made the world about her seem unstable.

Indeed, riding fast enough to keep up with others was not like the practicing rides around the smooth-stone courtyard behind her house or even the street leading to the caravan route. She held the leather reins tightly and pressed her legs against the side of her mount.

The eight year old Ishmael, first born of the family and named for his father, called, "Mary, don't be afraid."

"I'm not," she called back.

"You are too! You're holding on too tight. Jericho won't buck. Just pat her on the head—like this." He patted the white spot between his own animal's ears.

"Yes, like this," Solomon joined his brother in the demonstration, rubbing the long nose of his mount.

Mary laughed. "Nice Jericho," she said. She slowly copied the movements of the two boys. Jericho's ears wiggled. She pulled her hands away quickly. The ass brayed. Mary leaned back and almost fell off. She regained her dignity and balance, saying, "Nice Jericho. That's good, Jericho. I think we'll both get to understand each other soon."

The blazing sun shone down upon the broad plains of Esdraelon. As clouds moved across the sky the land was patterned with floating shadows and light. The caravan stretched into a long line, avoiding the brown hills to the south which rose in Samaria. Evening shadows were welcomed as the travelers encamped beside the Jordan River. Family groups gathered to prepare for the evening meal. The children played running games and splashed at the river's edge to work off the energies restrained by the tiresome ride.

After the men had fed and watered the animals they clustered together, sharing views of the political situation in all of Judea. A few Roman soldiers in their short tunics and glistening helmets stopped briefly to inspect travel papers. Immediately the conversations changed to the market values of merchandise or weather conditions. When the soldiers rode on, the dissatisfaction with the Roman occupation again became the subject of discussion.

Mary alternated between helping the women with preparing vegetables for the huge pot of stew and keeping track of her three charges. As she gave Rachel the package of food, which her mother had prepared, Mary said, "Isn't the scenery beautiful?"

"Just a lot of rocks, if you ask me. Never changes, year in and year out."

"But the flowers—"

"Flowers? The tares you mean?"

"No. The wild flowers. The anemones. The fields of yellow mustard and blue flax. It's so exciting."

"Oh, I suppose. But frankly, I'm anxious to get this trip over with. It is so tiring and boring." She walked away to stand behind the men to listen to the diatribe against the Romans.

Welcome cool breezes swept down from the mountains and after everyone had eaten they rolled themselves in their cloaks or bedrolls. A few men remained about a fire to protect the sleeping camp from wild animals and the many marauders who preyed on unsuspecting travelers. Mary lay marveling at the multitude of lights in *Adonai's* canopy, the star-studded sky. She checked the small boys lying on both sides of her, said her prayers, and slept soundly.

By sun-up the caravan was moving again. Because of the age-old hatred between the Samaritans and the Galileans, many caravans followed the east bank of the Jordan River. After fording the shallow water, the group began the steady winding up and around craggy hillsides covered with green cedars and pines mingled with the delicate lacings of trees leafing out in different shades of green, pink and deep red. The air was brisk, the asses frisky, but the children were quiet as the early rising left them less than the talkative, active youngsters of the afternoon before.

Mary welcomed the interlude of quiet. Even though many of the campers said their morning prayers, they were hurried and intruded upon by the constant shouting of the camel drivers and the many who did not share in the worship of the Lord. She thought of her father's slow, deliberate devotions dedicated to their God: the laying of phylacteries, the ceremonial washing of his hands, the donning of his white wool prayer shawl with its many blue fringes.

Then, she marveled at God's hand in getting her to Elizabeth's. She tried to recall the last time she had visited Ein Karen. *I was only about eight at the time and that is over half a lifetime to me. I do recall the quiet dignity of Elizabeth and the wonderful flower garden that surrounded her house. I didn't know the names of the flowers and bushes but Elizabeth knew every one and she had patiently recounted them to me. I remember that the yard seemed like a big bouquet of colorful blossoms and green leaves with the two-story house sitting like an alabaster carving in its midst. I wonder if Elizabeth still has the garden.*

She thought of Zechariah. *I wonder if he will take me into Jerusalem with him one day to see the temple where Adonai dwells.* She conjured God housed in the building that was supposed to be the most beautiful building in all the land—maybe in all the world. *Adonai* deserved the finest. He had made the mountains and the rivers—the River Jordan which now and then she would see from the road. He had made all the people who were traveling to somewhere with her. She wondered about all the places these strangers came from and were going to.

The caravan grew as other people, who were going to Jerusalem to observe the Passover, joined them. The small inns along the way were always filled, so that it was necessary to sleep out in the open. Mary was glad that the weather was moderate. During the third day the temperature cooled noticeably as the parade of animals climbed over the rocky ridges toward Jericho.

The children joining the group would laugh when they heard the name of Mary's mount." "Jericho, Jericho," they sang along. "Jericho rides to Jericho." Mary enjoyed hearing the children laugh. It made the journey easier and the days much shorter.

On the fourth day they neared Jerusalem. In the distance Mary could see the white building with its golden trimmings: that famed temple she wanted to visit. Briefly, it dominated the view then disappeared. The road divided and her group broke away from the caravan to go the seventy furlongs southwest of Jerusalem. The road they followed was narrow and twisting, not packed tightly as there were no camels making daily journeys up this incline. Their small caravan had the five asses they were riding plus four with bulging bundles strapped to their backs and sides. Mary wondered how the small creatures managed to keep going with such loads, but they plodded along on their tiny hooves through the rutted clay until the small village of Ein Karen loomed ahead.

Mary's heart pounded. *What will Elizabeth say when she sees me?*

Will   she be happy for the surprise, or will she know that I am coming? Did Gabriel tell her about the Messiah's birth?

"Isn't that Zechariah's house ahead, Mary?" Rachel asked.

"I think it is. But it's been a long time since . . ."

"Does your cousin know you are coming?"

"No. We had no time for a message, but mother said that she would be home. It is Passover time and Zechariah wouldn't be away from the temple. Also, Elizabeth must stay to feed her goats. She raises a special breed for the long hair. She weaves, you know. My parents thought I could learn some weaving and embroidery while I'm here."

"Wonderful pastime. And so necessary. Up in these hills it gets very cold."

"There she is now—in the road—waving to us." Mary thought *Elizabeth has not changed much since I last saw her standing in her hillside garden. However her gray hair has turned white. Her skin looks almost translucent.. Ah, but her eyes. Their bright flaxen color matches my mother's. How very much alike the two cousins look.*

Rachel spoke up, "I must be imagining this—but it looks like your cousin is with child—a miracle at her age, I would say," Even with the loose flowing ungirdled gown of mauve linen, Elizabeth's condition was obvious.

"A miracle, indeed," Mary said.

Chapter Nine

Elizabeth Greets Mary

As the small caravan stopped before the house and Ishmael helped Mary from her mount, Elizabeth came to greet them.

"Mary, Mary," she said as she walked toward them with out-stretched arms.

"Cousin Elizabeth," Mary said as she kissed the older woman on her smooth flushed cheek.

The boys insisted on helping Mary into the yard and leading Jericho to the courtyard. After the new family had been introduced, Mary received a tearful goodbye from little David as her friends left and continued on their way down the road toward the cluster of white houses in the distance. When they were alone Elizabeth said,

"Blessed are you among women and blessed is the fruit of your womb. And why is this granted me, that the mother of my Lord should come to me? For behold, when the voice of your greeting came to my ears, the babe in my womb leaped for joy. And blessed is she who believed that there would be a fulfillment of what was spoken to her from the Lord." [1]

Mary was overjoyed with the greeting. It made the meeting with Gabriel less a dream. The reality became more sure as Elizabeth held her hands against her well-rounded mid-section. Mary placed her own hands on her own flat, youthful body. Smiling and crying tears of joy at the same time she answered,

"My soul magnifies the Lord, and my spirit rejoices in God my Savior, for he has regarded the low estate of his hand maiden. For behold, henceforth all generations will call me blessed; for he who is mighty has done great things for me, and holy is his name. And his mercy is on those who fear him from generation to generation. He has shown strength with his arm, he has scattered the proud in the imagination of their hearts, He has put down the mighty from their thrones and exalted those of low degree; He has filled the hungry with good things, and the rich he has sent empty away. He has helped his servant Israel, in remembrance of his mercy, as he spoke to our fathers, to Abraham and to his posterity forever." [2]

"Mary, we are both blessed," Elizabeth said. The two women stood clutching each other, crying tears of happiness.

"Come, let us go inside to tell Zechariah."

"He is home now? I thought he would be at the Temple on the eve of the Passover."

"My husband has retired, Mary. He is unable to carry on his duties."

"He is ill?"

"He has been unable to speak since Gabriel talked to him. He disbelieved the word of God that I would conceive. As you see, he should not have doubted," she smiled. [3]

Unmindful that the two women had entered the room, the old man stood, rocking back and forth, with outstretched arms calling soundless prayers. He was dressed in a dark woolen robe, untrimmed, unbelted. His white prayer shawl all but covered his face. Mary could see his white beard quivering in the narrow opening. He did not look like the proud and stately Zechariah she had once seen in all his priestly finery.

Elizabeth said, "He spends his days asking forgiveness for doubting God's word. Being unable to serve his post has depressed him."

"I understand, for I, too, doubted Gabriel's words. God miraculously made it possible for me to come to you when I needed someone to talk to. Surely God will correct his speech problem when your little one comes."

"You have great faith, Mary. What do your mother and father say? I'm sure they are very proud."

"I couldn't find a way to tell them or my betrothed Joseph. I thought Gabriel would speak to them, but he didn't."

"What made you think of coming here?"

"Because Gabriel told me of your condition."

"I see. We shall have a glorious visit. My babe is due in three months. I have made arrangements with a neighbor woman to be with me. Since it is not considered proper for an unmarried young girl to attend a birthing that will be a good time for you to return home. By then we will know how to tell your family."

"I am certain that God will resolve any problems that I might have. Already he has solved my returning to Nazareth. Ishmael and Rachel are to come after me about that time."

"It will work out well," Elizabeth touched the praying man's shoulders. "Anna's Mary has come to visit us," she shouted. He looked startled. She turned to Mary and said softly, "I don't know why I shout at him. He can hear even if he can't speak."

The old man held out his arms to embrace Mary.

"She is with child, too, my Husband. Gabriel spoke with her also, telling her that she had been selected to carry the Messiah."

"And I, too, was afraid and doubted his word," Mary assured him, then added, "But when the wonderful glow and warmth spread over me I knew the spirit of the Lord had been with me. I am still amazed to think that I have been chosen."

Elizabeth nodded her head as she answered, "The Lord sent you here for a purpose, Mary dear. He will unfold his plan before long, I'm sure. Come let us get you settled in your room while I have the servants prepare our evening meal. I know you must be very hungry and tired."

Mary laughed and said, "Four days riding on an ass is not restful. But is was worth all the discomfort to be with you."

"Wait here," Elizabeth said as she left the room. "I will send someone to help you"

Zechariah returned to his prayers when his wife left. For the first time Mary looked about the room. She had not wanted to appear impolite by staring at the richly furnished house. How often had she heard her father rail about the costly living of the priests. He complained about the way the common people were required to give their first, their finest animals and crops to the temple, knowing all along the priests would take their offerings for themselves. He would always end with a shrug of his shoulders saying, 'It has always been so. *Adonai* gave the laws to Moses and he himself chose the tribal priests.'

Mary thought, *It's my father's own fault that he did not become a priest himself. Life would have been so much easier for our mother if he had taken his rightful place beside his elder brother.*

Mary touched the silken draperies which hung beside the openings in the walls. Soft and expertly woven, a blue pomegranate design made a wide border along the hem. Burnished lamps held by heavy cords hung from the ceiling. What a contrast the white walls and ceilings were to the drab, smoke-stained walls of her own home.

I think I will ask Joseph to white-wash our walls. And we'll have draperies. How much cheerier our house would be with some bright hangings to go with the pillow covers I've already finished. Then the thought rushed over her. *What if Joseph does not take me into his house as his wife?*

Before she could worry further over that question Elizabeth came through the door saying, "Come now, we will go up to your room. Nadia will help you unpack."

Mary was surprised to see the girl, Nadia, with burnished black skin who was probably only a few years younger than Mary herself, wearing a simple shoulder to floor white gown. A slave! Mary was shocked to learn that Elizabeth had a slave. The thought of one person owning another bothered her. *How could my cousin who has been so honored by the Lord stoop so low?*

She followed the silent servant girl up the wide marble stairway to the spacious room she was to call home for three months. Nadia poured water into a shallow bowl for Mary to freshen her face with cool and fragrant splashes. When Mary was finished the girl motioned for her to sit on a low bench. Weary from the long day Mary welcomed the soothing bathing and oiling of her feet. She longed to question the dark-skinned maiden about how she had become a part of Elizabeth's household. But she refrained, silently reminding herself *My mother taught me that I should never ask personal questions of strangers. That would certainly show poor breeding. Even though I come from a poor carpenter's family I must practice good manners. Always!*

Mary was awed by the evening dinner placed on the large table by Nadia and another young girl who might have been Nadia's sister.

Mary's mind churned. *How can I sit here and eat this food while two slave girls serve me? When should I tell Cousin Elizabeth how I feel about this?*

"Mary," she heard Elizabeth call her name. "Mary, you seem to be miles from us. Are you troubled?"

This is no time to say that I disapprove of slavery, Mary thought. *That would be impolite. But later, perhaps tomorrow will be the right time.* She looked up and smiled as she looked upon Elizabeth's face. *This woman is not evil. I am not being a good guest, criticizing how my hostess lives.*

"I was thinking of something else, my Cousin. Forgive me."

"You are tired from your long journey. Now eat. Food will make you feel much better."

The table was spread with white linen and lighted by white candles in branched candelabra. There were small plates and silver bowls for each person. When Elizabeth unfolded the generous square of linen beside the small bowls and placed it across her knees, Mary unfolded the linen square beside her own bowls. Elizabeth wiped a smudge of food on her hand onto the cloth. Obviously these were to be used to wipe off fingers soiled by food. Mary thought of her own family's mealtimes. *A common bowl to dip bread from bubbling stews. We lick our fingers to clean them. Sometimes the boys make noisy sucking sounds of approval if the foods are particularly savory. Our poor parent's scold them to no avail!* She smiled.

A platter of roast lamb was held for Mary to choose a piece for her own plate. *We seldom eat meat. Roast lamb is served only for holidays and special guests. I must be an honored guest!*

Later Nadia served slices of red melon. Not sure how this should be eaten Mary waited for Elizabeth to begin. When her hostess looked up and saw the look of bewilderment she lifted a narrow wedge of the melon to her lips and said, "Very good. Very sweet."

Mary nibbled on a thin slice and quickly used her linen cloth to wipe a trail of pink juice from her chin. "I have never tasted a red melon before," she said. "It is very sweet and juicy."

"Watermelon. Melon—imported from Egypt."

Imported from Egypt! How could my cousin prepare this feast in such a short time? Perhaps father is right. Priests do eat like royalty all the time.

Feeling the warmth of being well fed, Mary said, "That was a wonderful dinner, Cousin Elizabeth. After eating rather sparsely, I might say crudely on the journey, this has been a delight to be served so beautifully. The roast lamb was a real treat. I feel very honored that you consider me so special."

"Special? Of course you are special, my dear. Very special. I do hope you had enough to eat. As we have aged our appetites seem to have lessened and we eat very lightly in the evening. However, I do have a bite now and then and I know I shouldn't. Sometimes I get hungry for the oddest food. Who would desire green olives?" Elizabeth chuckled as if enjoying a private joke. "No one eats an olive before it is ripened and black. But now I love the green ones cured in brine."

"I've heard that women with child occasionally crave unusual food."

"I am proof that what you have heard is true."

Mary laughed. "I hope I don't desire something rare and difficult to find."

"You'll know soon enough."

Darkness fell over the house with sudden shadows. Elizabeth touched lamps and candles with the flame of a candle from the table and light flickered all around the large room located in the center of the house. Mary paused by the doorway and longed to sink into one of the padded divans along one wall.

Elizabeth said, "I think we both need rest. Especially you, Mary, after your long journey. My husband and I have become accustomed to retiring immediately when night comes. We are early morning folk. I must be up and about with my animals at dawn." She clapped her hands and as if by magic Nadia appeared from behind a door. "Nadia will prepare your bed."

Again Mary had the urge to speak to Elizabeth about her aversion to slavery but decided the time was not right. She kissed Elizabeth on the cheek and bowed low before Zechariah then followed the black girl up to the second floor,

Where did the girl come from? I don't recall ever seeing anyone with such blue-black skin.

When they reached the room Mary asked, "Nadia, where is your home?"

"Here," the girl replied.

"Where are your parents?" *Indeed what kind of parents would they be who would sell their child as a slave?*

"No mother. No father," she replied as she held out a white cotton gown similar to the one she herself was wearing.

Mary took the gown. "I'm sorry, Nadia," she said.

"Oh, I am very happy here," the girl replied. She turned to fold back a coverlet on the low bed. Mary dropped her own blue robe to don the white one then lay upon the bed and thought, *If the girl likes being owned by Elizabeth, what can I say?*

With a small linen-covered pillow tucked under her head Mary relaxed and sank into the soft padded mattress. *What a contrast to the thin reed pallet I sleep on at home.*

As Nadia smoothed a coverlet over her supine body, Mary said, "You make me feel like a royal princess."

Nadia smiled, bowed low, snuffed out the light flickering from the small oil lamp, and left the room. A soft glow from the lighted stairwell filled the door way and then disappeared when the household settled down for the night. In total blackness Mary's prayers to *Adonai* drifted and faded as her mind plunged into a deep sleep.

Chapter Ten

Zechariah Teaches Mary

At dawn the next morning Mary heard Elizabeth's voice calling out names. With a start she sat up and for a moment she was lost in a strange white room. The sun rose suddenly and blushed the room with pink. Mary went to the door of the balcony outside her room and watched black and white goats come running to Elizabeth as she called their names.

Mary gave her morning thanks and immediately dressed to join her cousin. She helped carry grain and water and watched the older woman pull milk from swollen udders. Even with expert tutoring Mary could not keep a steady stream of the rich milk flowing into a jar.

The newborns bawled out their protests for being kept from their mothers. Mary caressed and hugged them, not being discouraged with her first goat-care efforts.

Mary loved the crisp mountain air. She stretched her arms high and wide as if to gather in all the beauty and freshness of the morning. She marveled at the flowers in full bloom that grew in among the vegetables of the neatly kept gardens. She could pick a bouquet at the same time she helped with the gathering of cucumbers and leeks. The garden which her mother labored over in Nazareth was puny compared to the lushness of this mountain retreat. She was familiar with searching for tender leaves on mustard plants but she was amazed at how much greener the local ones were than the Nazareth variety.

"Your garden is bountiful, Cousin Elizabeth. We all work very hard to help our mother but her plants do not flourish like these."

"The secret of good gardening is this," Elizabeth said as she scooped up the dung of her animals and threw it on a compost pile of cuttings and weeds. "What your mother needs is a herd of goats." Elizabeth laughed and the sound was good.

They went into the house and found Zechariah had taken up his prayer position at the far end of the central room. He was deep into his meditations and made no sign that he saw anyone pass by him.

"It breaks my heart to see my husband so low in spirit instead of rejoicing that we are to have a child," Elizabeth said.

As they walked from room to room Mary was impressed with the handiwork that Elizabeth had created. Her mother had always spoken of her cousin's magic with the needle but now Mary was seeing it all for the first time, through the eyes of a woman who was about to start her own new home. Mary talked about Joseph and how she had already loomed pillows and tablecloths to brighten his house.

Even at that early hour the house was neat. Mary thought of how her parent's house looked until noon: *Trying to get the morning meal, getting mats rolled and in place, nagging at the boys to pick up soiled clothing. Confusion reigns during the first hours before the boys leave to study or to play. There is no doubt that children create lots of work.*

Mary turned and saw Nadia and the other black girl straightening pillows on the bench along the wall.

Certainly servants make life more orderly, Mary thought.

Elizabeth seemed to sense Mary's concern. She said, "I suppose you are wondering about Nadia and her sister living here with us."

The direct statement startled Mary. *How did you she know? Is my distaste so obvious?*

"Yes," Mary answered quietly. "I have wondered why you of all people would have slaves."

"Nadia and Rhodia are not slaves. Their parents were brought here from Africa by a very cruel and ruthless Roman official who did not like children to be around his house. He ordered them taken away to be sold. Their mother brought them to the temple, hid them in some laundry and left them hoping someone would rescue them. They were about four and six years old as well as we could tell. Zechariah brought them to our house where they have been part of our family ever since. Unfortunately our skin colorings are not the same and they have not been received with friendliness in this community."

"I might have known, my dear Cousin. You could never own a human being no more than I could."

"The girls know they are free and may leave at any time but they are still so young they choose to remain here with us. Even though that cruel man has returned to Rome, taking his stable of slaves with him, including their parents, the girls seldom leave our house as they fear all Romans. They insist on being treated as servants since no one seems to question our having two African girl servants and do not bother them. But I would rather they were considered my daughters."

"How sad for them to be deprived of their own flesh and blood," Mary said. "I cannot understand why people dislike others simply because they look differently. Someday there will be no hatred between people because of color. I feel this is so, just as I am convinced that some day women will be treated as equal to men. The old ways that allow women to be bought and sold, wed and divorced upon whims of men must go. We have to begin to fight for freedom, Elizabeth. Our sons will treat everyone with respect. They will know that no one is superior. Only our Lord, our beloved *Adonai,* is superior. That is our mission, my Cousin. A new world must begin with us."

"Mary, the more I talk with you the more I understand why you were chosen to bear the Messiah. You are right. A new world will begin with us through our sons."

They went into a room larger than the one Mary had slept in and Elizabeth said, "Come, let me show you the new robes I had prepared for this season." Elizabeth knelt down beside a wooden chest. As she unfolded richly decorated robes she said, "This is the first time that my husband has not gone to the temple for Passover. It broke my heart to see him so low in spirit instead of rejoicing that we are to have a child."

"Did you embroider these yourself, Elizabeth?" Mary touched a garment hesitantly. The older woman nodded and smiled as she held to her breast a robe of white linen edged with golden pomegranates.

"Mother says you are an artist with the needle and she hopes that you will teach me. Mother is very good at weaving and making our garments but she has little talent for difficult stitchery."

"Your mother has been very busy raising a family. I had no

children to demand my care . . . and love," Elizabeth said softly.

"Mother said that she felt it upset you whenever she was with child, just wishing that you might have one of your own."

"I must admit that I was jealous of your mother. I sinned in feeling that way. It wasn't that I didn't want her to have children, it was because I longed for a baby so much. I prayed and prayed to our Lord, and I cried because He did not listen to my prayers . . . when all the time He heard and I did not understand that I was to be a part of His plan. Now I am overjoyed that my son is to be the messenger to proclaim the Messiah."

"To think that we both have been chosen," Mary said, shaking her head slowly. "It is almost unbelievable."

"So, now we must make the most of the time He has made possible for us to be together," Elizabeth said, returning to the folding of the temple garments. I feel sure that one day my husband will want to wear these again. I shall keep them for him. I will spend my hours making new ones, even more beautiful, for our son who is destined to become a priest too."

"I do not believe that our Lord will expect our sons to be robed like priests or princes, my dear Cousin. If He had, He would have given the nurture of His children to royal families."

"I did not think of that, Mary. How wise you are."

"Nor do I believe that our Lord sent me here to learn to stitch well."

"Oh? What then was His purpose?"

"All my life I have longed to write . . . to be able to record important things I want to remember . . . to pass on to the future perhaps. My father taught me to read the Torah but he feels that a woman has no need to write or cipher. He says a woman should learn to cook and keep a family."

"True."

"Have you never yearned to read or write as your husband does?"

"No. I have never felt that need. I am very busy with womanly tasks. I have used my talents to glorify our Lord with the keeping of the temple robes and cloths. The Torah is covered with my stitchery. I have tried to clothe those whose needs are great. With my gardens, my goats and my needle I have little time to think of writing."

Mary looked into the blue eyes which were so much like her mother's. "Elizabeth. I believe this is all a part of *Adonai's* great plan. I truly believe that He has made His priest Zechariah unable to speak, forcing him to retire from his temple tasks, because it was destined that I come here so that I might learn from him."

"Why?"

"The Messiah must know basic skills to understand the word of our Father, our one God. He must be ready to lead others when the time is right. I have been given the responsibility of rearing him. We cannot wait until a rabbi is available and willing to teach him at the Nazareth synagogue. Nazareth is small and has limited educational opportunities. If we lived in Jerusalem my son could be sent to the Temple priests but He chose Nazareth for his childhood."

"I had not thought of that, Mary. I will speak to my husband. Both of our sons must know the words of our Lord."

On the morning of the third day Elizabeth spoke to Zechariah before he began his silent lamentations. "My husband," she said. "Mary wants you to teach her how to write."

No, no, no he shook his head and walked away. Mary followed him and said, "My dear Zechariah, do you not see that this is all a plan of our Lord? All these unusual events in our lives are tied to a miracle. You see I believe it is wrong that girls are not taught the skills of reading and writing. My father taught me to read the Holy words of the Torah and I am the only girl my age that I know who can read. But my father does not believe it necessary for any woman to write. I feel strongly that both Elizabeth and I should know how to read and to write. We must know these things in order to rear our holy children. Who knows what demands will be made upon our knowledge?"

Elizabeth nodded her head as Mary pled her case and then spoke up enthusiastically. "Think how wonderful it would be for Mary and me to exchange notes occasionally, to share our family happenings."

"Please, Zechariah." Mary pleaded. "I believe that Gabriel came to you as he came to me. There is a reason for his telling me about Elizabeth and your future son. Don't you think so?" She smiled and took his hands in hers.

He could not resist Mary's pleas. Unable to argue with two

women, especially since he could not speak his own reasons for refusal, the old priest at last gave in and began the daily lessons.

Gradually his depression lifted as he spent each morning teaching the mysteries of both the Aramaic and Hebrew letters. Sometimes Nadia and Rhodia would watch the women practice forming letters with pointed sticks in smoothed sand. Often the two girls drew pictures in nearby sand and pretended they too were learning to write, but they did not have the deep yearning to learn that drove Mary and they drifted away from the teaching area.

In a short time Mary and Elizabeth were scratching words on shards of pottery, then they practiced on wooden tablets covered with thinly spread wax on which they scraped words with sharply pointed wooden styli. When they became more skilled their patient school master taught them how to mix lampblack, resin, and olive oil into ink. Then he taught them to cut reeds at an angle, and where to slit them to hold ink for use on papyrus. Without his voice to explain he pointed to objects to give them names. He illustrated movement by acting out words. The mornings became games of charades. The three looked forward to each session. The teacher was pleased with the progress of his students. He no longer spent hours mouthing soundless lamentations.

For each lesson the two students inscribed list after list, first in Hebrew then in Aramaic. They wrote notes to each other to judge and to be judged. A broad smile from Zechariah told them when they had written all the words correctly. He had them copying the words of the Torah and David's Psalms. Mary's grasp of his teachings amazed both Elizabeth and her husband. Both were convinced that this visit had been a part of *Adonai's* grand plan.

In the afternoons Elizabeth helped Mary make a gown to wear for her wedding. At first Mary protested but Elizabeth thought it a very good exercise in sewing. With that finished they prepared swaddling cloths for their infants.

"We'll be ready when our times come," Elizabeth said.

"Why are babies wrapped tightly with these bands?" Mary asked.

"As far as I know, it has always been done in this manner." Elizabeth answered. "A baby's neck is very weak at birth, you know, so this protects the child and ensures straight limbs."

They kept the loom shuttle flying as they transformed flaxen threads into fine linen squares and strips. They wove Elizabeth's special goats' hair into small blankets to snug about the tiny bodies they were expecting.

"It gets quite chilly here even in the warm months, so blankets are needed. Certainly you will need several warm covers for your child as he will be born in the winter season. Think of me, your cousin Elizabeth, as you use these to warm our Messiah's little feet."

"I know that I shall be thrilled when I, too, will feel the movement of my child within me, as you do, my Cousin. That will make him even more real to me."

"Indeed it is a satisfying moment—especially the very first time. Now my little one is becoming very impatient with his confinement," she smiled as she rubbed to dislodge a hard knot in her side.

Mary had hoped to visit the temple while she was in Ein Karen but the days slipped into weeks and months. Even though she was busy, Mary became eager to return to Nazareth. Her love for Joseph nagged at her constantly. When the three months were at the end, Zechariah oversaw the bridling of Jericho, and the bundling of Mary's things ready for the portage animals. It was a tearful Mary who bid her hosts goodbye when Ishmael and Rachel came for her.

As they walked together to the waiting mini-caravan, Mary kissed Elizabeth and then Zechariah on both cheeks and said,"

"How can I ever thank you enough for all you've done for me?"

"Mary, dear, you must tell Joseph when you get home," Elizabeth said. "Remember, he will have an important part in raising the child."

"But what if he does not believe me?"

"You have trusted in the Lord and have not been disappointed."

"You make it sound so easy, Elizabeth."

"It will be, my dear. I know, for I denied the truth for five months fearing I was too old to bear a child. I worried that it could be false in payment for my jealous feeling for your mother and her lovely family. But the Lord heard my prayer of need, as He will hear yours."

The shouts of "Mary! Mary! " by three boys echoed all the way from the road to the house. The boys clamored toward her, gathered around to help her mount and then ran back to their own animals eager to start on the journey.

As the small caravan began the slow movement down the rutted lane, Elizabeth called, "Please bid my cousin Anna and her husband Joachim glad tidings."

As Mary waved in reply Rachel rode up beside her and said, "I'd say your cousin is about due."

"Anytime now," Mary smiled and nodded.

Chapter Eleven

Home! Home to Joseph!

The journey home was more tiring than the journey to Ein Karen had been. Summer's heat was unrelenting, even in the mountains. No rain had fallen to lessen the dust, and there were no cooling breezes in the evening to revive the tired travelers. Mary was delighted when they crossed the Jordan at Pella. With Mount Tabor rising in the distance she knew that they were nearing home. Never had a sight been more welcome than the low white houses of Nazareth.

"Promise you'll come see me," Mary said as she hugged each one of the boys who had been her charges for the past four days. They waved to her as she left the caravan at the crossroads where she had joined it three months before. Rachel and the boys remained with the other riders while Ishmael accompanied Mary down the lane to her home. She tried to assure him that she would be able to find her way until he reminded her that many of her bundles were loaded on one of his asses.

Mary thought about going by Joseph's house and then she decided she should go home first which was only seven furlongs from the turn-off. She pressed Jericho into quickening her dainty footstep-staccato on the cobblestones.

When the three animal caravan stopped at the cottage door, Mary called out, "Mother,"

Anna and Joachim ran out to greet their daughter. Instantly she was surrounded by the children of the neighborhood who were playing near the house.

Amidst the shrill childish shouts, her mother cried, "Mary, you're home! You look wonderful, my child. You've put on weight and your face is fuller. Indeed your trip was beneficial. I'm so glad to see you. We've missed you, dear."

"I missed you too, and I do feel wonderful, Mother." She kissed her mother and then her father on both cheeks. "And how is Joseph?"

"Well, lonely of course. We had him here to eat with us several times. Jacob died last month, so Joseph has been sad. Losing both parents so very close together has been hard for him."

"And I was not here to help him in his grief," Mary cried. Her mother held her close to her breast as she wept.

"You could have done nothing for him. Jacob's heart gave out. I think it was grief over his dear Ruth. He did care for her over her long illness, you know. Joseph will be delighted to see you, of course."

Ishmael and Joachim unloaded Mary's bundles and after a round of pleasantries, Ishmael left to join his family.

Mary turned to go down the road. "I'm going to see Joseph," she said.

"That wouldn't be proper, Mary," her father said. "I will go tell him to come here. You'll want to wash before you see him."

"Do I look that bad?" she laughed.

"No, but you're dusty."

"And what could you expect after riding four days in a caravan?" her mother said to Joachim. She turned back to Mary, "I know you haven't eaten. We just finished so I'll get something for you while you ready yourself for Joseph."

Mary gave Salome the promised silk scarf, one that Elizabeth sent to the young girl. The two boys were excited about the wooden shepherd's flutes which Zechariah made for them. They ran out the door, blowing, trying different notes from the new instruments. To Anna Elizabeth sent a piece of bright wool and a length of striped cloth, for Joachim a robe.

Her mother never ceased to ask questions. She wanted to know about the trip, Elizabeth and Zechariah. She was shocked when she heard about her cousin's expected baby.

"How can that be? I know Elizabeth is past child-bearing age."

"The Lord works in mysterious ways," Mary answered.

"Indeed. Well, perhaps, the Lord answered their prayers sent up to him faithfully all these years. But it does seem strange that her husband should have been stricken dumb just because Elizabeth was to have a child."

"It seems that the angel, Gabriel, spoke to him and he did not believe that such a miracle could happen. His speech was taken away because of his lack of faith. But he's very thrilled about his child. Now he believes the words of Gabriel that this boy is destined to be a prophet to prepare the way for the Messiah," Mary said.

"And you believed him? Just like that Zechariah to make out that his child would be someone special. He always did think he was better than anyone else—except of course the High Priest and the Lord himself."

"Mother, that wasn't a very kind remark. I think he is a very pious and sincere man."

"You don't know how he made fun of your dear father's body saying he didn't look like he belonged in the family of Abijah and then he ridiculed him because he would not stay with his studies for the priesthood. And his house. Always had the best. Taking things away from people that they brought to the temple for worship. Ate like a king at their house, while your poor dear father has labored so hard."

"Mother, you aren't being fair. Cousin Elizabeth raises fine animals for wool and milk. She has a wonderful garden which grows a variety of vegetables we don't ever see around here. Besides, I believe Zechariah talked with an angel because . . . ."

Joseph came through the door at that moment and Mary forgot all about defending Zechariah. She ran to Joseph and he took both of her hands in his. He looked down at her as if he could never see enough.

"Mary, my Mary, oh how I have missed you!" Mary could see the love in his eyes and she knew that hers were shining back with the same devotion. Their hands clung together, not wanting to let go.

"If I had known you were coming I would have baked a honey cake and we would have had some meat instead of this vegetable stew." Anna fussed around refilling Mary's bowl. "Would you care for a bowl of stew, Joseph?" she asked.

Neither Joseph nor Mary heard a word the older woman said. They walked out into the small courtyard where Jericho was tethered.

"How did Jericho behave?"

"Like a lady should," Mary laughed. The world was perfect this night. The air was warm, the flowers sweet, the stars bright in the sky. She was home! Home with Joseph. Still holding hands, they sat on a bench facing the low brick stove where Anna had cooked the evening meal. Amber sparks were tossed from the red charcoal buried in gray ashes, like fireflies flitting in the darkness.

"I was so sorry to hear about your father, Joseph. I'm sorry I wasn't here to be with you when you needed me."

"Yes, I missed you so much then, but I missed you every minute of every day, my darling. It seemed the time for you to return would never get here. I'm so happy to have you home, " Joseph said.

"I missed you, too." Mary put her hand up to his cheek and watched lights reflecting in his eyes as sparks drifted above the dying fire. "I have something to tell you, Joseph. I tried to tell you before I left but could never get the right moment with you. Elizabeth made me promise that I would tell you this immediately upon my return."

"You sound very serious, my Mary. What have you been holding from me all this time?"

"I am with child, three months now."

"But, my beloved, that cannot be. I have never touched you—though I have wanted to many times."

"I hope that you will believe me, Joseph, that I have known no man."

"You mean there have been many?" his voice broke.

"No—No. I mean there has been no man. I have had no man touch me."

"How, then, do you know of your condition?"

"I have missed my flow three months."

"There are many illnesses that can cause that, I understand. Even worry. Did you tell your mother? I'm sure she will know."

"No, Joseph. An angel of the Lord spoke to me and the Spirit of the Lord came over me."

"You have been imagining this, Mary. You can't expect me to believe that you are with child and still have no man touch you. Do you think I'm naive?" He withdrew his hands from hers and moved from the bench to stand in front of her.

"No, Joseph. You are not naive. I find this very difficult to explain . . . it has been very difficult for me to understand also . . . but I know that it is time for me to tell you. I will be showing soon."

Joseph pulled at his hair with both hands. "How can this be

happening to me? I would have staked my life on your faithfulness, Mary. This is a terrible blow to me." He wiped his eyes with the back of his hand.

She stood up and put her hand on his forearm. "Joseph," she said softly. "I understand your disbelief. You have a right to disown me and divorce me from our betrothal vows."

"And let you be the next victim of a village stoning?" He pulled his arm away abruptly.

"I can go away. I can return to Elizabeth's and I would be welcome. She, too, is expecting. She insisted that I return without fear because she believes that you care enough for me that you will not cast the first stone as required by law."

"I could never stone you, Mary. But I cannot say the child is mine and admit that we are guilty of adultery. That will tarnish our parents' honor. The shame . . . is . . . ." he broke into tears.

"There is no shame, my beloved. I have remained a virgin."

"Then the baby is imaginary?"

"It is real, Joseph. I am carrying the Messiah for the Lord. The angel Gabriel came to me on the day Rebecca was stoned."

"You are very sick, Mary, although you look so well. You are very sick in the head to imagine that. You were under great pressure and sorrow that day. You had an hallucination. It didn't happen, Mary. You have imagined it, that's all. If you stop to think how foolish this idea is: you are not of royal blood. The Messiah will not come from common stock."

"I am not of common stock, Joseph. Your father and mine bragged that we both come from the royal line of David, many generations back." She put her arms to him and he turned away, looking up toward the sky, blinking his eyes to hold back his tears.

"I don't know what to do. I cannot let you be stoned; I cannot marry you and admit a guilt that is false. I think the only way that is open to me is take you away somewhere and see to your safety. [2] There you will be able to live with no stigma. I must go home now, to resolve this dilemma that you have presented. The Lord knows I love you, Mary, but I cannot believe that you are with child and no man . . . ."

He left without touching her or saying goodbye.

When she returned to the house her mother asked, "Where is Joseph? He left so quickly."

Mary did not answer but went to her room and knelt in prayer.

"*Boruch ato Adonai I have lost Joseph. If he does not believe me, who will?*" She lay looking up at the stars and in spite of being bone-tired from riding Jericho all day, she could not go to sleep.

Chapter Twelve

Joseph Returns to Mary

With dawn's first lilac and pink blush of the eastern sky, Mary rose quietly, dressed, and stood her rolled sleeping mat in the corner. She carried her sandals and tiptoed barefooted, to avoid awakening her sister who was sleeping beside her. Noiselessly she made her way to the courtyard. She was drained of tears and did not want to talk to anyone, feeling the need to find again the peace that she had known before Gabriel had spoken to her. Taking a ewer from the small cupboard beside the door, she walked toward the well. With every step she thought *I have to make plans for my future. No doubt, I will have to go back to Elizabeth's.*

If Joseph does not believe me, my parents will not understand either. Hadn't my mother once said that the Messiah would be born to royalty? Everyone believes that. But then, didn't I stated my own doubts to Gabriel?

As she walked past the plane tree, she saw that spiked, green globes had formed and were hanging on every twig and branch of the tree insuring a plentiful harvest of rich, brown nuts to roast in autumn fires. She paused at the jutting boulder where her whole world had been tossed topsy-turvy and she prayed again, as ardently as she ever had prayed.

"*Boruch ato Adonai*, My Blessed Lord, lead me in the path that you want. I gave myself to you as your handmaiden. Now, please tell this your obedient servant what to do. Cousin Elizabeth said that I should not worry that I would be cared for.

"But Lord, I do not want to be cared for by anyone but Joseph. All my days I have dreamed of him as my husband, and now he thinks I am deranged . . . full of an imaginary child.

"My Lord, I know this is no dream. This is real. I am about to have a child with no father. You are his father but you do not manifest yourself."

She waited for an answer, for a slight rustling of the scant bushes, a bird, a gentle breeze perhaps, but there was no movement, no sound. The moon was still in the sky, pale as the sky, to remind her of her sleepless night.

She was at the well before any of the other women arrived. As the sun tipped over the horizon, bathing rocks and land in rich gold, she plunged her jug into the deep pool of clear cool water. A soft rustle of dripping water gurgled from the filled ewer as she unloosened the rope from its handle. A voice in the distance called, "Mary, Mary." She paused and listened as it called again.

Bouncing off rocky walls, the voice sounded hollow. It was a voice willing her name to travel a distance. Then she saw Joseph running up the path, stopping to cup his hands as he shouted.

"I'm here," Mary answered but she knew her words did not carry to him as he stopped at the boulder to cup his hands again. She ran toward him and as they met he enfolded her in his arms. She knew her prayers had been answered. Joseph believed her and wanted her.

With his lips buried in the soft curls of hair released when her scarf fell, Joseph said, "Mary, I love you. I could never live without you. Last night I walked for hours after I left your house. I cried and I cursed. I didn't know what to do. I decided to divorce you quietly and send you away, seeing to your care wherever you might go. I even thought of joining you there later, but I could not bear to have anyone in Nazareth scorning you."

"Joseph, I didn't sleep one wink last night knowing how you felt and I decided that whatever you thought best for me I would do without protest. I arose at dawn and came here hating to face a day of questioning as I knew my parents wondered what had happened between us. I didn't even talk to them last night for fear I would cry."

"Mary, last night I experienced a miracle. Gabriel came to me in my sleep and told me of the Holy Spirit and your son who is to be called Jesus. He said this was to take place to fulfill the prophecy that a child would be born to a virgin and his name would be called Emmanuel, God is with us." [1]

"Facing Gabriel is a terrifying experience," Mary said.

"I found it frightening in a dream. I awoke shaking first with awe, then with joy that I was to be a part of the life of the mother of the Messiah. I take that as a very grave task, an honor almost overwhelming to think of the trust that is placed with me."

"Oh, Joseph," Mary said. "I could ask for no greater joy than to share my life with you."

"I wanted to come to you immediately but decided to wait until sun-up. I was impatient with the sun, it rose so slowly. When I felt that you would be awake, I went to your home and your mother was surprised to find you gone. She looked for the water jug and decided you must have gone to the well early, before the day's heat flared."

"Joseph, it was on the day that Rebecca was stoned, at this very place in the road, that I met Gabriel. Beneath the feathery leaves and blue flowers of the fitches in the patch across the way, you can see lily plants standing there with yellow, withered leaves and small green knots on the end of the stems. That day they were aflame with sweet-smelling red blooms. I knelt there as the spirit of the Lord came over me. Then I returned that afternoon to fill the water jug I had forgotten, the sight and fragrance of the red lilies convinced me that I really had met the spirit of the Lord, as Gabriel said. When I went on to fill my jug, a white dove fluttered from a willow tree and then flew away. It was so beautiful."

"Look, Mary, a white dove rests just above your head on the small bramble bush growing from that crevice in the rock. "

Mary turned and lifted her arms toward the small bird but it flew away. Mary smiled as she felt the presence of her Lord.

"Let's go tell your parents so that we may be wed immediately." He took her hand and turned back down the lane.

"Wait," Mary said. "I mustn't forget the water jug this time."

"Give it to me," Joseph said. "I'll carry it for you.. " Taking the jug from her, he tucked it under his arm in manner that spilled water down the front of his robe. Mary laughed.

"That is a woman's job, my husband-to-be. Soon, we will be meeting other women going to the well and they would not understand. Here, give that to me and I will not spill a drop." She placed the jug on her head and led the way down the narrow path, walking slowly with the rhythm of a woman whose body is in perfect balance.

When they reached the widened part of the path they walked side by side. Mary greeted the women who passed them, acknowledging that she had been gone quite a while, that she was glad to be home, and yes, that she was feeling much better now and that she would be married soon. They all knew Joseph and greeted him cordially.

The cobblestone, house-lined street afforded them more opportunity for a private conversation. Joseph said,

"Mary, you seem worried about something. What is it?"

"My parents. Do you think the Lord wants them to know our secret? I thought all along that Gabriel would come to mother to tell her, but he didn't. He came to you instead. And he came to Zechariah and shared his plan with Elizabeth. Why didn't he tell my parents?"

"I don't know. Perhaps you are right. As soon as possible I will take you to my home and declare us man and wife before two witnesses."

"My mother will not take this lightly. She is planning a big wedding. She wanted it in the autumn when good food and wine are plentiful for a large celebration."

"We can't wait until Tishri, Mary. We will have to marry now. We must insist. I can persuade your parents, I feel sure."

Anna was in the street awaiting their return. "I see you found her," she said. "You look happy as if you have patched up your lovers' quarrel."

"We had no quarrel, my future mother-in-law. My bride-to-be was very tired from her long journey. We had many plans to make and she became weary. We are going to the rabbi now to discuss the terms of the *ketubah*."

"Ah yes, I spoke with him not long ago. We are planning the wedding party near the time of Feast of the Tabernacle. Since you are their last son, I know your dear mother and father would have wanted to have a big celebration. I have been saving up to do the honors for them."

"We have decided not to wait until the harvest season, Mother," Mary said. " We will be man and wife as soon as the papers and witnesses can be arranged."

"What do you mean. No wedding! It would be a disgrace to have no nuptial party. Wait until you father hears this. He will not allow it, Mary."

Gently Joseph touched Anna's shoulder as he leaned close to her and said in a sad, soft voice, "I am very lonely now after the death of my dear father. He made me promise that, I would bring Mary home as soon as she returned from Elizabeth's. He loved her like a daughter. How can you deny the last wishes of a dying man?"

"And you are happy, Mary? You are happy not to have a wedding like all your friends have?" her mother asked.

"I will be happy where ever Joseph is, my Mother. Oh, so happy."

Chapter Thirteen

Preparations for the Wedding

A faint sound outside her window awakened Mary. Her mother was poking the fire in the brick oven. The fragrance of baking sweet cakes filtered into the room along with the acrid odor and faint flickers of light from pitch torches burning in the courtyard. Mary knew that her mother was determined to have a wedding feast whether the bride and groom wanted it or not.

The previous afternoon, her father had been sent to find a lamb, a rarity so far past the lambing season. Proudly he had brought one home, bleating and wriggling to break his tight grasp. Now it was secured in the little shelter where Jericho was tethered. Once during the night, Mary heard its cry and went out to calm the frightened creature. It made her think of the baby goats which she had helped Elizabeth feed. Until the time she had to return home they had followed her about the yard as if they were her own pets. She missed them.

This is my wedding day, she thought. *My wedding day.* The words sang in her ears. *Today I will belong to Joseph and he will belong to me. Today we will be known as a family of Israel.* Her heart pounded. She could ask no more of life than to be as happy as she was at that moment.

"*Boruch ato Adonai,*" she whispered. "My heart bursts with joy. I have more happiness than one woman can hope for: marrying Joseph and mothering the Messiah, Your Child. Let me be worthy of this moment of great joy, my Lord."

With a sudden rush of guilt, knowing that her mother was working so early to make wedding delicacies, Mary rose, smoothed her gown and hair, then hurried to the courtyard where Anna was kneeling, stoking the fire. In the dim pre-dawn grayness, the red glowing coals, flaming blue and yellow tongues, splashed light over her mother's face.

"My Mother," Mary said softly. "You are arisen too early. It is not yet dawn."

"I know, but I have so much to get finished for this evening. The honey cakes plus the fig and nut goodies. Then the lamb . . . ."

"That lamb is a dear one, Mother. I cannot bear to have it killed. It is so frightened. Didn't you hear it bleating in the night? I came out and held it until it calmed down."

"Your father went to great effort and expense to find that lamb for this evening. The rabbi will prepare it for us this morning." Anna emphasized the words "effort" and "expense" with a sharp poking of the coals. Then she added, "Since there is no woman in Joseph's household, it is proper that I prepare our feast for him."

"But we don't need a feast, Mother. Father and Levi are witnessing that Joseph is taking me to wife. We made no plans to have a celebration. I will go home with my new husband as soon as the witnessing is over."

"Surely you will not deny your father and me a small party to honor the starting of a new family—our first born—our own daughter's wedding? Joseph's mother and I had planned such a fine celebration and I promised Ruth . . . ." Her voice cracked, "Now I have to break that promise because Joseph is too impatient to wait," she said as she poked the fire vigorously. Red sparks scattered and flew at her. She retreated quickly from the oven opening.

"Mother, do not be angry with Joseph, it is difficult for a man to live all alone. He has been housekeeper for his father and now he has no one. Would you deny . . . ?"

"It seems he could have waited a while until your engagement period is over or until we had time to get in the proper provisions for the occasion. Men! Always thinking of themselves!" Anna slapped a bit of dough on an oven tile.

"Joseph is not just thinking of himself, Mother, I assure you," Mary said as she poured water in a bowl and began washing her hands.

Joachim looked in the doorway. "So early, my Wife and my Daughter? Even the sun has not awakened." He yawned and stretched his arms as if to awaken his own sleeping body.

"Mother is anxious about the wedding. I am telling her that Joseph and I do not expect a fancy feast."

"If we cannot have a rightful wedding celebration," her father said. "You must indulge us for having a quiet family feast."

"But a lamb, Father. It is so dear, I don't want it killed to eat."

"Nonsense! Lambs are born to be eaten. Now if you two insist on rising before the sun is up I must get on with my morning prayers as I cannot sleep with all this clatter."

"Now who is making a clatter?" Anna asked. "I was quietly baking sweet cakes . . . ."

"And I came out to scold her," Mary laughed. "Let's not quarrel on my wedding day. If it is a feast you want, I shall help you."

The day went quickly. The children all became involved in the preparations. The boys brushed Jericho until her coat shone, then they tied bright yarn tassels all over the leather harness. Proud of their work they took turns riding the little ass, shouting merrily to anyone within hearing distance to look at them.

Anna stopped them with a sharp, "Quiet! Get off that animal and give it a rest. It will be worn out before we get it loaded with Mary's things."

"It will take more than two boys riding her to wear down Jericho, my Mother," Mary laughed. This was a wonderful day for her: her family lovingly working together. Salome insisted on fetching the water. Over Mary's protest the younger girl won out.

"You must pack all the things you received at your betrothal party, Mary," Salome said. "You can do that while I go to the well. After all, I went to the well all the time you were gone." She picked up the large ewer and ran out the door.

Joachim returned from the rabbi's house. "Here is the lamb," he said to his wife. Mary did not protest but shuddered in revulsion when the pink flesh of the animal was dropped upon the work shelf by the oven. She thought about the warm animal it had been only a few hours earlier as she cuddled it in her arms. Tears came to her eyes but she said nothing and went to gather up the things she would need to take with her to her new home. Joseph's home. Their new home.

She heard her father saying to her mother, "I have prepared the lamb for the spit. I knew Mary would be distressed to see the newly killed animal, although I'm sure she will eat of it after it is roasted."

"I doubt if Mary eats anything today. I remember how excited I was on my wedding day. Food is not on a bride's mind, I assure you, my Husband. But we must continue. Prepare the fire and the spit. The boys are being pesky, trying to wear out little Jericho. They may be given the task of turning the meat and that will keep them busy. You must speak to them and make them feel that is a very important job."

"It is," Joachim said. "If that lamb should be burned no telling what I might do."

Mary sorted through all the things she had woven, sewn, or embroidered all the days before her engagement. A young girl of Nazareth spent her whole childhood preparing herself for the day she would marry, as it was a disgrace to go to a groom without new household goods made by the bride herself. She added the things she had received from the guests at the betrothal: bowls, pitchers, linens, skeins of wool and flax, all packed inside the copper pans her cousins had brought from Caesarea. One of her prize gifts was the pair of embroidered slippers which she had saved to wear on her wedding day. How long ago that betrothal party seemed, so much had happened to her in the past three months. Her life had changed from being an excited bride-to-be to one concerned about the secret life she carried within her.

She lifted from the chest the leather purse which held the two hundred dinars Joseph had brought to her betrothal party that night. Two hundred dinars for her to keep as her own. She remembered how Josie had said jokingly for her to keep that money hidden, always, so that she would never be a pauper just in case Joseph changed his mind about wanting her as his wife. "Men do that, my dear Mary." She had said. "The Law gives a man the right to divorce a wife any time he wants to. That isn't fair but that is the Law. So remember to keep this money safe in a secret place."

All the women had laughed as Josie gave her advice, but the laughs were mere chuckles. Mary and every woman present knew that Josie had spoken the truth, but as Mary looked around the group that had gathered about her, she saw no man who had taken advantage of that law. Most of the couples who were their friends, relatives, and neighbors had been wed many years. Most of the men, like her father, had become so accustomed to the ways of their wives, and had such a hard life making a living, paying the taxes to the Romans, to King Herod, and to the priests, they found little need or time to seek new wives.

It seemed only the wealthier women had that problem to worry about. *Being poor has some advantages. Indeed I feel no concern about Joseph's seeking another wife and discarding me. He loves me . . . as I love him on our wedding day.*

At the very bottom of the small chest she found the folded, white pennant which had flown outside their door to inform passersby that there was a joyous celebration of a betrothal in the house. It was an open invitation to enter and join the celebrants. She laid the pennant aside. Salome could use it whenever she became betrothed. She picked up the sheer veil that Joseph had given her that night. She thought *I should put this with the pennant for Salome. No, I will wear it myself with the simple dress I made with Elizabeth's help. The veil will make me look and feel like a bride even if only the family will be here to see me.*

Lying inside the white pennant was the folded bright woolen girdle, with its metal buckle embossed with the lion-head symbol of the House of David. Joseph had worn that night of the betrothal and had given it to her during the formal ceremony to pledge their troth. She placed it with her things so that she might return it to her husband this night.

She unfolded the length of embroidered, sheer silk which Rebecca's mother had pressed upon her. There was no time to make a wedding gown from it now. Mary held its softness to her cheek. Tears welled as she thought, *Rebecca might have worn the gown made of this. Life goes on and we can't look back at what might have been.* Mary wiped drops of tears from the material as she laid it with other uncut cloth, waiting for the time for it to be made into something useful.

After she had finished packing the things she wanted to take with her, Mary joined her mother in filling the round flat baskets with honey cakes and sweet meats of dates and nuts to be handed out to the children so they might remember this wedding of Joseph and

Mary. There would be plenty of neighboring children to be treated. The youngsters always gathered wherever sweets were available. Joachim brought in a large, tightly-stretched skin of wine.

"Father," Mary said, "we do not need that much wine. Levi and Josie are coming as our only guests."

"But you never know who might come. I invited the rabbi and he may casually mention the event to someone."

"Father, we don't want a big wedding. It is not proper at this time of bereavement for Joseph. It will be depressing enough for him to have to appear in his mourning clothes as he cannot forego his duty to his father."

"Can I help it if some friends drop in to pass the time of day?" he shrugged. "I must get the fire started to roast the lamb."

Anna brushed some flour from her hands, a movement she often used to wipe a problem from her mind. "Your father is happy, Mary. He is proud of his fine new son-in-law. It's just like him to invite everyone he saw on the street today," she said. "Don't worry about what your father does. That is one thing you will learn in time. When a man makes up his mind to do something he can find all kinds of excuses to make it seem reasonable. There is little hope of changing his mind. Come now, it is time for you to begin to getting yourself ready."

Her mother poured heated water into a large kettle used during wine making while Mary hung blankets to create a private corner of the courtyard where she might take her ceremonial bath, She reveled in the luxury of the warm water trickling over her body, cascading to the pool at her feet.

Anna lifted a corner of the blanket and entered, saying, "Allow me to soften your skin and refresh you with the special oil I made for you, sweet smelling as crushed honeysuckle blossoms."

Mary turned her back toward her mother, but Anne's quick eyes scanned the dripping body. She poured the oil over Mary's smooth shoulders and swiftly rubbed the unguent over her back and then, as if Mary were still a small child, she slid her hands over her breasts and shielded torso.

"Mary," her mother said, "do I feel the swelling of your body as that of a woman with child?"

Mary hesitated, hunting for words. She had not planned to reveal her secret on this day, her wedding day.

"Look at me, Mary." She grasped Mary's shoulders and turned the girl's body around.

Mary's eyes were downcast and a rush of blood flooded her face. "Yes, my mother, I am with child."

"That sneak—that Joseph—robbing our child—our Mary of her maidenhood before time. No wonder he wants to be wed immediately, or did you have to threaten him for defiling you?"

"My mother, do not blame Joseph. He is pure and he has not defiled me."

"Surely you are not saying that Joseph is not the child's sire—that some other . . . ."

"I am saying that Joseph is not to blame."

"Who took you then—a cad here in Nazareth or someone in Jerusalem? Maybe one of those young priests in Jerusalem. I hear things like that happen. Tell me and your father will lead a scourge party of revenge. Our Mary deceived! And what of Joseph? Does he realize that some other man has beaten him to his marriage bed?"

"I have told him."

"And he will have you anyway?" Anna gasped, holding on to the wall, ready to cry out. Mary knew the time had come to tell her secret.

"I am not blemished, my mother. I am the virgin who is carrying the Messiah," Mary said softly.

"The Messiah!" Anna spit out. "Foolish girl. Who told you that you were to carry the Messiah?"

"The angel Gabriel."

"An angel? You are daft, my Daughter. You do not have to make up such a tale to cover your indiscretion. Probably this all may be laid to a young priest of the temple, as I said. While you were under a spell, the awesomeness of the temple, richness of some temple wine, and the guile of a glib tongue made you believe that you would carry Our Savior." Anna pulled at her hair until it fell from the tight knot at the nape of her neck. She did not notice her dishevelment. "Oh, that Satan works through the slick words of his deceivers! And to think it would happen to my child." She looked up to the heavens and waved her hands about in a wild manner as if to scream out her pain. "Oh Lord God, why have you put this stain upon us? We have been defenders of your Laws always."

Mary put her hands on her mother's outstretched arms.

"Mother, I have committed no such indiscretion. I met no young priests in Jerusalem. I was so busy I did not even get into the city."

"Of course, I do not blame you if you lay with Joseph," she babbled on like a woman possessed, "You are betrothed. If you could not wait to consummate that betrothal, your father and I will understand and forgive you for sullying our good name. We know it was difficult for you two, knowing each other, loving all these years. Now with your father and I —well—we never saw each other until our wedding day." She began to cry softly, "Oh, times were different then. We honored our parents—and did not break the Law. But young people today don't care about the Law. They don't care about their parents." She wailed and tears washed her cheeks.

"Mother, I tell the truth, I carry God's child."

"Of course, my dear. Every child is God's child," she sobbed as she stepped back and let the curtain fall. "Hurry now. You must get dressed for our feast."

Mother doubts my revelation. How could she question my truthfulness? I've always told the truth. Never once in my lifetime can I recall lying to my mother--or to anyone.

The joy of the day was diminished by the knowledge that her mother did not believe her. At that moment Mary knew that few people would believe that her child was the Messiah. She would have to keep this fact buried in her heart until the Lord chose to reveal His Son in his own time.

Chapter Fourteen

The Wedding

Mary listened to her father's booming voice welcoming Levi's family, then the rabbi and his wife. As the voices of gathering guests grew, she knew an invitation had been extended to many, even to some who were not close friends. She wished that Joseph had been able to get the word to some of his brothers and sisters, but most of them lived a distance from Nazareth. She knew that Joseph would be surprised to find the house and courtyard filled with wedding guests rather than her family.

Mary heard her mother crying softly on the other side of the curtained door. She pushed the curtain aside and touched the shoulder of the sobbing woman, huddled behind a stack of mats which had been moved to allow more room for guests.

"Mother," Mary said gently," do not be distressed over what you have learned this afternoon. You are carrying on as though I should be held in disgrace. I am not disgraced—neither is Joseph—nor is our family. We have been honored. Believe me. This is a joyful wedding day. Please smile and go help father greet the many friends he has invited. It is good that you have prepared so well."

Her mother rose without saying a word. She wiped the tears from her cheeks and soon Mary heard Anna's sandals slowly scraping along the floor. Then came the pseudo-joyful voice of her mother calling out, "Levi and Josie." Mary smiled. *The crisis is over. Mother understands.*

Mary finished tying a pale blue ribbon to hold her hair in place when Salome came in, bringing daisies from the patch at the well. The younger girl tucked the white flowers into the band creating a floral head piece.

"You look so beautiful with your daisy crown, my Sister."

Mary kissed her on both cheeks and thanked her for her thoughtfulness.

Salome tied a ribbon about a slightly wilted bunch of daisies. "Carry these for me as you go with Joseph," she said.

, At the door Joachim's loud voice boomed, "Behold the bridegroom comes."

"Hurry, Mary, didn't you hear Father? Joseph is almost here," the younger girl said.

"I heard," Mary answered. She kneeled as she handed the veil to her sister. "Please put this on my head."

Joachim came to the curtained door and said with ceremony in his voice, "Mary, my Daughter, your bridegroom approaches."

"Thank you, Father," she said as she peeked through the narrow opening. She watched her father rush to the door and the guests moving back as Joseph entered. Mary was surprised to see him in a betrothal robe, gaily striped with gold, red, and blue. A white wool tallith, which Anna had given him at their betrothal, was draped over his shoulders. He had discarded his drab, mourning sackcloth, had washed the ashes from his head and generously oiled his hair and beard. The two most important men in Mary's life hugged and kissed each other on both cheeks. Unsmiling, Anna stood nearby. Joseph saw her and engulfed her in his arms.

"Greetings on this happy day, my almost Mother-in-law. I bring my cedar branch to mingle with my bride's pine bough." He laughed as Anna stepped back, then fell into his arms again, weeping with great sobs.

"Do not cry, my Bride's Mother. This is a time for joy. You and I have cried together at my father's and my mother's funerals so let us rejoice together at this my wedding." He dried her eyes with the hem of his sleeve. "Look what I bring for you." He handed her two shining needles in a silken case. These will make your lovely sewing even more beautiful."

"May the Lord bless you, Joseph," she said in a tearful voice. "You are so good."

"And you my almost Father-in-law, I bring you a woolen girdle of regal purple to denote my respect for your word." He bowed low as he handed the brilliant sash to Joachim. Then he called out loudly,

"Where is my bride? I have come for my bride. Where is she hidden? Bring her forth that I might see what I have bargained for."

Joachim parted the curtains and took Mary's hand. "Behold your bride, Joseph," he said.

The chattering guests and children quieted as Mary appeared wearing a pale blue robe. The sheer veil, hiding her blush, was held in place by the ring of white daisies. The flowers of the crown and her hand bouquet were wilting but she did not notice. She saw only Joseph standing at the door, waiting for her to join him. Standing beside him her father was proudly holding high a bough of pine which she knew he had cut from the tree that had been planted at her birth. With ceremony Joseph presented the cedar branch from the tree that his own parents had planted so long ago.

The rabbi called out, "Where are the witnesses to this marriage?"

"Here." Joachim pushed Levi ahead of him. Levi took the branch of cedar from the groom, and the greens were arched above the couple.

"Where is the marriage agreement to present to the bride?" the rabbi asked.

Joseph handed him the papyrus roll itemizing the worth of his gift he had prepared to give his bride. The rabbi nodded, made great ceremony of perusing the roll he and Joseph had prepared the afternoon before. The list was small as Joseph's time had been cut short by six months. He had planned many gifts but had no opportunity to either make or buy them. The ceremoniously garbed old man nodded again his approval of the agreement and handed it to Mary, who without reading it, pressed the roll tightly in her hands with the flowers.

She lifted her blue eyes to meet Joseph's dark ones and holding the flowers and roll in one hand, placed her other small, soft hand in Joseph's work-worn one.

Joseph said, "I hereby take Mary, daughter of Joachim, to wife." He lifted the veil as the green boughs were entwined. "Never has my bride been more beautiful, is this not so?" he asked of all those attending.

The gathered guests shouted their approvals and then pelted them with grain, to insure a fruitful union. Children banged sticks together and wildly shook tambourines. Mary's two brothers blew shrill notes on their new shepherd's pipes.

Joseph put Mary on Jericho, then holding high a flaming pitch torch, he led the parade of well-wishers to his home. Each guest carried a parcel, which contained either food for the feast, or part of Mary's household goods which she and her mother had hastily gathered together. They all sang praises from the psalms of David and new voices added to the din as the torch-lit parade grew along the way. When they reached Joseph's house, Joachim and Anna quieted the children and in turn the adults by reminding them that while this was a day to rejoice, Joseph was still in mourning and should not be subjected to great merrymaking.

At the door Joseph lifted Mary from Jericho saying, "Come Mary, I take you into my home as my wife."

"Hear, hear," Joachim and Levi repeated. "Joseph takes this woman, Mary, to wife."

Taking over the role of host that would have been Jacob's, Joachim turned to the crowd behind him and said, "Come, now, let us feast and celebrate the forming of a new family of Israel."

Immediately, Anna took charge of laying out the food: platters of the sliced lamb, baskets of fresh-baked bread, olives, figs, pomegranates, dates, nuts, raisins, and honey cakes. Mary marveled at all the things her mother and friends had provided on such short notice. Joachim playing host, poured the first wine into a cup for the bride and groom to share, and gave a toast,

"To our new family of Israel may it be fruitful." The bride and groom drank and dashed the glass to the floor. Toast after toast followed with Joachim pouring the wine freely.

Joseph was spirited away by playful friends and Mary sat in a chair while her friends lounged on cushions at her feet. The merrymaking went on for hours and Mary wearied of it, wishing that she and her new husband might be together. But she knew there was no hope that the customs of ancient days could be broken. The bride must wait patiently for the groom's return. Her friends were to keep her company. But the girls became tired and bored. Some napped, others left. Since there had been no formal choosing of bridal attendants, no one felt obligated to remain with her during her vigil. Mary was relieved when the pranksters ceremoniously returned her groom.

At dawn the house was emptied of all but Joseph and Mary. After a loving embrace he led her to his wedding gift for her, a mattress on a platform at one end of the room. The furniture had been moved around to make room for the many people milling about and Mary had not realized that the soft, wide bed was Joseph's gift to her.

"I ordered this from Kafda, the sailmaker, months ago. I spent this morning arguing with him that he should let me have one completed for another order. To get it today I promised him a fine cedar chest for his daughter's coming betrothal."

"It is so soft," Mary said as she sat on the edge of the wide pillow-mattress and patted it on both sides of her.

"Washed wool fleece," he said proudly. "Try it. Lie back and feel how much better it feels than a mat."

Timid and embarrassed, she lay across the wide bed as Joseph knelt to remove her embroidered wedding slippers.

Chapter Fifteen

Mary Receives a Gift and a Message

Feeling the soft fullness of the wide mattress, Mary stretched her arms and legs. Until she had visited Elizabeth, she had never slept on such a bed, and she had wished then, that she could have one for her home. But she did not allow herself to hope that she might ever own such luxury.

She thought of Joseph's tender embraces after everyone had gone, and she sighed with resignation at his insistence that she remain pure and untouched, until she would give birth to the child. She understood and loved him more deeply for his concern of her and reveled in the memory of his warm arms enveloping her just before he went into the other room to sleep upon his solitary mat. She longed to share the wonderfully soft nest he had given her but did not tempt him to forget his pledge of protection.

In the morning Mary heard Joseph stoking the fire. She hurriedly threw an extra robe about her and rushed in the kitchen to take over her wifely duties of preparing the meals.

"My Husband," she said, savoring the sound of the words, "My Husband, may the Lord bless this our first morning together."

Joseph was squatting before the fire. At her greeting he stood and came to caress her, holding her close to him. "The words, my Husband, are like honey to the bee, my Wife. Again, I shall praise the Lord for your nearness. Did you sleep well?" he asked.

"Like on a cloud. But I felt guilty having such a wonderful bed while you were lying on a thin mat."

"Sleep comes to me anywhere, my dear. My bones are not fragile like yours."

"Fragile, am I? I am a woman now, and as strong as any woman in Nazareth. Indeed! Do you think I am still a small child? She stood straight but her eyes could only peek over his shoulder. She stretched on tiptoe to make herself appear taller and looked up to see the amused smile on his face and the twinkle in his eyes.

"You are a very old woman, my Wife. How could I have been talked into marrying such an old hag?" He held her close and whispered, "Mary, Mary, how proud I am to be your husband."

"Then, go about your duties, your ablutions and your prayers, my Husband." Mary said. "I am the wife of this household and must do my wifely tasks."

She took a ewer and poured water over his hands and left him to the laying of his phylacteries before his morning prayers. She did not realize the problems she faced. She was unfamiliar with the household. She had to search through the bundles which the guests had brought over the night before in order to prepare their first meal alone.

So quickly had they set up housekeeping the utensils were assorted left-overs that Joseph had been using plus a few given to her by her mother. But she went about preparing the morning repast. She wanted it to be perfect.

She had planned everything: she had put aside some sweetmeats from the wedding feast and packed them in a small package with her clothes and she had brought enough starter dough for baking the morning bread. But the fire was too hot and burned the thin cakes; the pulse was too dry and over salted. It seemed that every thing went wrong and she was in tears by the time Joseph was ready to eat.

"I so wanted it to be perfect," she sobbed as she sucked on a finger, red and blistered by the charred bread.

He comforted her and offered a basket of freshly picked figs.

"We can feast on these, " he said. "These are the first of this year's crop. My mother planted the tree years ago when it was only a small whip with two leaves, now it shades the courtyard and gives us our bridal fruit. I'm sure my mother would be pleased."

"I should not have let myself get so upset, but I really thought I knew how to do everything. Now I know that I only helped my mother, she really did the cooking and baking. She was teaching me how to be a wife, and often I did not listen or watch as carefully as I should."

"No doubt she had the same problems. I, too, am finding that there are many things my father knew about wood that I did not try to learn. We all seem to think our parents will be with us forever . . . but when they are no longer here we find there are so many questions we did not ask."

During the first few days Mary dusted Joseph's mother's loom where it stood in the corner, untouched since her death. Mary strung strong, unbleached cotton threads and using some strips of dyed worn clothing, she had brought with her, she began to weave rugs to lay about on the flat stone floor. This task was among the first to be started. It was important to her because it seemed that no matter how many sweepings she made, grit ground under her sandals or caught between her toes. Joseph was impressed with the bright new rugs and bragged about his new wife's cleverness with the loom.

Mary placed new bright pillows on the wide bed, which had a place of honor in the main room of the house. She polished the table that Joseph's father made for his own bride many years before. Mary wove a fine linen cloth to protect its patina.

As time went by, relatives and friends forgave Joachim and Anna for not inviting them to the wedding. Anna painstakingly explained how Joseph needed a companion after the recent deaths of this parents. Gradually, gifts of pottery, baskets, and linens came to "the new family of Israel." Mary was delighted with every gift, but even more, she cherished the good wishes and love that each one brought.

Every morning Mary practiced her writing skills by scratching letters on a pot shard or by moving a stylus in wet clay. She used the one piece of papyrus, which Zechariah had given to her, for copying the prophecy of Isaiah which was so close to her.

> "Therefore the Lord himself will give you this
> sign. Behold a young woman shall conceive and
> bear a son, and shall call his name Immanuel." [1]

During the warmest days of the season, many women in Nazareth wore loose and ungirded robes, so Mary's condition was not apparent to the casual observer until about her sixth month. She spent many days with her mother, sewing, making small garments for her expected infant. Anna was solicitous about her daughter's health, giving advice freely: avoid green vegetables, salt food and fat; never take a hot bath for fear of a miscarriage, then reversing her own advice, warned that she must eat plenty of salt fish and mustard.

Her mother said, "Not that I believe it, of course, but they do say that the wearing of a dead scorpion tied up in a crocus-green cloth, and fastened on to the woman's skirt will guard against a miscarriage. And drinking powdered ivory in wine or water will help insure an easy birth." [2]

Mary laughed at her mother's words. "I don't need any magic tricks. My child will be protected from evil by his Father," she answered.

"Indeed Joseph is a strong man, Mary, and no doubt he will be a protective father, seeing after you and your child. You are so fortunate to get a forgiving husband. Never have I seen or heard of a man who attends an unfaithful wife as he does."

"Mother, Joseph knows that I have been faithful. He knows . . . ."

"He is a man in love who will believe any tale. But no matter, your father noticed your condition today. I told him nothing. He is going about bragging to anyone who will listen. Fruitful; he calls the two of you, bearing so soon after the wedding. He is boasting that he must be the grand-sire of twins, so big you are at three moons."

"We must stop him, my mother. He must know the truth. He will be the laughing stock when the child arrives. Everyone will know then, that he has been deluded."

"No. Not until the child is laid in his arms, will I let you tell him. He must not know of the shame you and Joseph have brought to our family. He will forgive you when he holds the child . . . and if it is a boy, he will proudly hold him while he is circumcised. No greater pride has a grandfather than to hold his first grandson for the cut of the ceremonial knife, and to be allowed to bury the foreskin in his own soil to preserve his family line in our beloved land."

"No," Mary said. "I cannot lie to my father by omitting the truth."

A loud rapping and shouting at the door sent Anna scurrying to see who was calling, "Someone! Anyone come to the door. I have a message!"

Anna was shocked to see Nathan, the silk merchant, standing in the road clutching a rug and holding a scroll. Neither Anna nor Mary had seen him since the day of Rebecca's funeral. He had never acknowledged the respectful kindness the two women had shown toward his daughter and they had not expected any thanks for their fulfilling the Law.

"Nathan," Anna said bowing her head in deference to his position in the community, "What brings you to my lowly home? Please do come in. My daughter Mary is in the courtyard and I'm sure it would please her to see you. She speaks well of your wife and before she went to Ein Karen she often called on her. I'm sure you know that."

"I know," he said, standing straight as if the task before him was difficult. "I must not tarry, but I have a message for your daughter, Mary."

"A message?" Mary joined them as her name was spoken. She bowed her head, in the same manner as her mother had. "Who would be sending me a message?"

"A woman who raises goats and weaves fine wool."

"Elizabeth!"

"As you know I am a merchant of fine fabrics and I deal with merchants from Damascus as well as from Jerusalem. One such trader perchance bought fine wool from her for a special order. Upon learning that his route home included Nazareth she asked him to carry this scroll and to seek out someone who could find a girl called Mary, daughter of Joachim and Anna. I accepted the honor to bring the scroll to you myself—in gratitude for your kindness to my daughter."

He handed the rolled scroll to Mary and then said, "I have wanted to speak to you, but my daily delays grew until I did not feel that my words of gratitude would be acceptable. I ask forgiveness for my slowness."

"We acted out of our love for Rebecca and for our one God and His Law," Mary said.

"Rebecca! My wife and I have not been able to speak her name" the man said. "The word is sweet and I was not able to say it for so long—knowing the terrible wrong I had committed on my lovely child."

"Do not be so hard on yourself, Nathan," Anna aid. "You thought you were following the Law."

"I was a proud, greedy man. Mary and you showed me what love meant and I was too hard-headed to admit my error. But I have changed. My wife and I have tasted the cup of bitter sorrow together and have learned about love."

"Perhaps it is the Lord who sent the messenger," Anna replied.

Nathan unrolled a rug as he said, "Mary, I heard that you were wed recently, and I bring to you this from Persia which the merchant had with him. Please accept a belated gift from us."

Mary handed the scroll to Anna so that she might take the rug. They both marveled at the soft, deep pile of brilliant colors blended and twisted into scrolled patterns.

"This is too great a gift," Mary said. "We expected no payment for friendship."

"This is no payment, this is a gift of friendship. The Greek word is agape, friendly love," he said as he stepped back into the sunlit lane. He bowed low, stretching his hand at his knee, in the manner of a slave bending before his lord.

The women bid him farewell as he mounted the white horse tethered to an olive tree near the walled garden.

"What a gorgeous rug for our home," Mary said.

"It will make everything else look poor beside it," Anna said.

"No. It will bring warmth and more love to our already overflowing house of love. I shall cherish it more dearly because it carries with it the joy of cleansing a man of guilt and sorrow. No one can know happiness and love if he has no peace within himself."

"The message," Anna said, taking the scroll in her hands. "What of the message from Elizabeth? If your father can't read it we will have to take it to the rabbi to read."

"No, my mother. I can read the script. Zechariah taught me to read and to write Aramaic and Hebrew while I was there."

"I thought you were to learn fine stitchery from Elizabeth," Anna said.

"I did that too . . . but . . . ."

"No matter. Read it then. I must know what is happening with our dear cousin." With the same confidence she had shown while studying at Ein Karen Mary began:

> "My dear Cousin Mary,
> Our child was born shortly after you left us. He
> is healthy and we named him as Gabriel had

instructed my husband."

"So, Elizabeth did have a child," Anna said. "At her age! A miracle!"

"I told you, Mother, but you didn't believe me."

"It is difficult for me to understand what has been happening. What else does she say?"

Mary read on,

> "My husband regained his speech and roused up
> the priests and the people when he declared our
> John was destined to be the prophet for the
> Messiah. Zechariah returned to the temple as a
> priest only to be slain by someone who didn't
> believe him. He died with his hands on the horn."

"Zechariah dead!" Anna cried out. "This will come as a blow to your father knowing that he could not be present to mourn his death properly. He always looked up to his eldest brother. I think Joachim was awed by his stature as well as his priesthood. He tried so hard but he never felt that he could equal his brother's talents."

"Oh, my dear Elizabeth," Mary cried. "They were happy to be blessed so late in life. What a terrible thing! We talked of our babies' futures, made clothes for them together. It doesn't seem possible . . . ."

"How sad for our cousin, and we were not there to mourn with her. What is she going to do now?"

Mary read on,

> "Some Essenes have been very kind to me and
> have offered refuge at their retreat. They believe
> Zechariah's message that our son was born to
> become a prophet, like Elijah, sent by our Lord,
> to prepare the way for the Messiah. These
> people are very devout about expecting a
> Messiah. I am leaving today to go to Qumran
> with them, taking baby John and my beloved
> goats. I will dedicate my remaining days to study
> and to the teaching of my son. I am certain that
> you will be doing the same. May our Lord bless
> and keep our Holy Sons safe. Until we meet
> again, give my love to Anna and Joachim and

their family. Special love to you and your Joseph.

Your Cousin Elizabeth"

"Praise the Lord for sending this messenger." Tears rolled down Mary's cheeks. She knew that she might never again see the woman who had strengthened her faith; who had given her solace and understanding; the woman whose husband had been sacrificed for her unborn child for proclaiming his kingship.

"Where is Qumran?" Anna asked. "I never heard of it."

"I don't know. Perhaps Father or Joseph knows."

Chapter Sixteen

Gold Comes to Joseph

Each morning Mary and Joseph followed the pattern which Anna and Joachim had firmly set in the young wife's mind. She tended the fire and baked the morning bread while Joseph went about his devotions. Now that she had stored all her own things and had rearranged the house to suit her needs, Mary became another Anna, so experienced were her hands at wifely tasks.

The excitement of the holy days of Yom Kippur, Sukkoth and Hanukkah were over. The days passed quickly and as Mary's time neared, the child's weight increased. Her steps slowed with the shortening hours of light. Evening shadows were setting in early when Caesar Augustus, Emperor of the Roman world, sent out an edict that all men, living within the empire, should report to their ancestral homes for a census. Members of the house of David were commanded to register at Bethlehem.

"It is a cold and rainy time of year, my wife," Joseph said. "I must go as the Emperor has decreed, but you are nearly ready to deliver, if I reckon the time rightly. You must stay here for your mother's care."

"I will go with you, my Husband. Do you think I would want my child to be born without you near?"

"But are you able to take such a journey? Bethlehem is fifty furlongs past Jerusalem," Joseph said. "Even in fair weather that is a good four-day journey."

"It has been said, my dear Joseph, that the Deliverer will be born in Bethlehem. Surely it is the Lord's work that the edict has been sent forth at this time so that the prophesies maybe fulfilled."

"True. So it has been written. I had forgotten."

"Yes," Mary said as she repeated the words of Micah:

"But you, O Bethlehem Ephrathah, who are little
to be among the clans of Judah, from you shall
come forth for me one who is to be ruler in
Israel," [1]

"It will be as you say," Joseph nodded. "Tomorrow is the Sabbath
and we shall leave soon after, so we may reach Bethlehem before the
next Sabbath. This will give me time to finish the work I have started
and perhaps collect some monies owed to me for past work."

"I'm sure my father will be willing to do what cannot be put aside.
He does not have to travel for the census. The Levis have no ancestral
home."

Anna argued about her daughter's proposed trip so late in her
confinement. Mary reassured her. "I do not worry, my Mother. My
Lord will not allow His Son to be harmed."

"It is a woman's place to protect her own young. I say a four day
journey on an ass is risking too much."

Joachim raged that Joseph would think of taking his pregnant wife
on such a journey. "It is cold. The days are short. The sun rays no
longer warm the air and ground. Surely she will become ill with the
lung disease if you insist. Have you no husbandly care in you?"

"My Father," Mary said. "I insist on traveling with my husband."

"You are so large now—you must have twins. Your mother and
I worry about you."

"Do not worry about me Father, I shall be well protected by our
Lord, our One God. After all I am carrying His Holy Child."

Anna joined them. "Yes, all children are holy in the Lord's
eyes—indeed." As Joachim left she whispered to Mary, "Do not talk
about the baby being the Messiah. Everyone will laugh at us—you
proclaiming to be carrying a holy child. Go if you must—but say
naught of this pretense of a Messiah. It is unbecoming to speak of
such a happening in the lowly family of a joiner. Everyone knows the
King will come from a royal family."

Mary cast her eyes down. She had thought that her mother
believed her since the day the message from Elizabeth came. To know
that she still doubted was disappointing.

"As you say, my Mother," she said. "I will not mention my child's
honor to anyone. I do not wish to cause you any worry. Let my father

assume that I am six months with twins if it will make life easier for you." Anna nodded and left.

Joseph was busy with his morning devotions when a loud voice calling, "Joiner, joiner," rang through the small house.

Mary moved the bubbling pot of porridge to the side of the stove and went to open the door and was surprised to see Benjamin. If he recognized her he did not mention her name but asked that Joseph come to him.

"My husband is busy with his devotions now," Mary said. "When he is finished I shall tell him you are here. Please come in." She stepped aside to allow him room to pass his immense body through the door.

"Tell him now that I am here to pick up the bridal chest I had ordered from his father." Benjamin's voice rang with authority. *How repulsive he is,* she thought, *so fat, so arrogant.* She retreated as Joseph came in, still wearing his shawl and phylacteries. As he walked he folded the white woolen square and began unwinding the black straps circling his arm.

"My father was unable to work due to his sorrow over my mother's death, so I finished it for him," he said. "I wasn't sure you wanted it after . . . ."

"True. I have no need for it now but I am an honest man who pays his just debts," he said. "I ordered it and I'll take it."

"The chest is in the workshop. I've kept it covered for protection, against the time you might call," Joseph said. "It is of the finest imported acacia wood, banded with brass straps and handles. Come, I will show you."

Benjamin turned to a Nubian slave, who was standing beside a cart pulled by an ass, and motioned for him to follow. The man and slave followed Joseph into the cave adjoining the room. The sight of the man with his contemptuous air and fine raiment made Mary feel ill. Even riding the ass on her trip to Elizabeth's had not caused her to feel so squeamish. She had been more fortunate than most women, not having that long period of morning sickness, but her repugnance at seeing the man responsible for Rebecca's death was so great she was forced to hurry out the door. The bitterness of gall burned her mouth and stung her nostrils as she was unable to control her nausea.

She returned to the house to wash the sourness from her mouth. She sank upon her bed and tears flowed as she recalled the sorrow of that terrifying day. She listened to the men as they walked out to place the chest in the cart.

Benjamin said, "That is a beautiful chest. I shall put it in a place of honor in my home to remind me of the sorrow my terrible temper caused. I have never had a moment's peace since that day."

"Do not use this chest as something to remind you of sorrow," Joseph said in his soft, gentle voice. "Use it as an altar to pray to our Lord for peace of mind. Remove the hatred from your heart, Benjamin. No man can live with hatred of himself. Forgive others as you seek forgiveness for yourself."

"May the Lord bless you with many sons," Benjamin said. "He has already blessed you with a faithful wife."

"And one who loves the Lord," Joseph said.

Mary heard the cart pull away and rumble down the cobblestone lane.

"Mary," Joseph called.

"I am in here, my Husband, lying down. I felt faint and needed to rest." She was ashamed to admit to Joseph that hatred had made her ill.

"Old Benjamin was so pleased with the chest he gave me more gold than my father had quoted. Now I have enough extra to buy another ass so that we both may ride together to Bethlehem."

Mary felt that she would rather walk than take money from Rebecca's killer, but then she reasoned that perhaps this was the Lord's way of helping Joseph. Jericho could only carry one of them, and that would make Joseph walk every step of the way. Besides, he was so overjoyed with his sudden acquiring a means of travel he did not even notice her reaction to the morning caller.

Chapter Seventeen

Jesus Is Born

Joseph named his new ass Jezreel. The animal was older than Jericho and well-trained for carrying fully loaded panniers. Along with the food and clothing needed for the journey, Joseph packed a few joiner tools into one of the bundles.

"I'll take some of my tools," he said to Mary. "I can always pick up a few coins to pay for our keep. We'll need to stay in Jerusalem until the time of your birthing purification."

Mary made up a bundle for her expected child: the swaddling cloths, a small sharp knife, and a piece of dried gut which her mother had insisted she put with her things. "Just in case . . . " Anna had said. Anna was always thinking ahead. Life had taught her to be prepared for any emergency. "Just in case" was one of her oft-used phrases.

As she put the folded, small blankets in the bundle Mary hugged the warmth of the soft wool to her and felt near to her cousin. She wondered if Elizabeth ever got to Qumran. Neither Joseph nor her father had heard of it. When she asked about the Essenes they knew there was a radical sect by that name but they didn't know anyone who belonged to it. Mary was certain that if these people did believe in the Messiah's imminent coming, they would find Him. She had no doubt that the Lord had made elaborate plans to fulfill the age-old scriptures. She did not speak of this to Joseph or to her parents but kept the thought buried in her heart.

It was an especially chilly day when Joseph and Mary left Nazareth, hoping to join with a caravan on the main road some miles away. Again the family walked to the crossroad on which travelers assembled to await a group coming from the north. The road was empty. Cold weather discouraged long distance trading.

In a way, this parting was a joyous occasion for Mary because

Joseph was with her, plus the knowledge that she was about to fulfill the prophecy of the Holy Word. Yet she was slightly apprehensive about that role. Last trip, her great concern had been getting to Elizabeth's and finding her cousin when she arrived. Then the weather had been warm, the flowers were in bloom, and she was part of a large group riding together for protection. Now, almost nine moons later, the weather had changed. Skiffs of snow bit into her cheeks and stung her eyes and it seemed that she and Joseph might be forced to travel all alone. She shuddered slightly as she remembered how the jackals had howled, and once the men had driven off a lion prowling about the camp. She pushed aside such worrisome thoughts. She knew she would be safe. Her cargo was too precious to be unprotected.

Joachim brought along a thick wool blanket and said, "Joseph, keep my loved one wrapped warmly so that she will return safely. I worry about her riding that ass even a few days in her condition."

"She is young and strong, my Father-in-law. I have no fear for she wants so much to come with me, I cannot leave her."

"Women! So stubborn. They do not have good sense most of the time," Joachim said clapping Joseph on the back. The two men laughed.

Anna pressed a small bag of coins into Mary's hand.

"I'd been saving these for your wedding but since we didn't use, you take . . . just in case." She and the children were crying. Mary tried to speak but couldn't get the words to form on her lips. She pressed her mother's hand and kissed her on both cheeks, then held her close.

"Mother, Mother," she whispered too softly for anyone else to hear. "I love you. I wish that you did believe that I take this journey to fulfill the scriptures. It grieves me greatly to know that you doubt the holiness of my child. I pray you will know sometime."

"My Daughter, I no longer fear for you as I know nothing can harm the mother of the Messiah. God be with you all the way."

"Thank you, my Mother, your blessing will go with me every moment."

After another round of tearful embraces with her parents, Salome, and the two brothers, Joseph lifted Mary onto Jericho and the two-animal caravan began wending its way down the lonely road. The early mists soon blotted out the loving group they had left at the crossroads and the two began the solitary journey, with only the clip-clop of their animal's hooves breaking the silence of the fog-shrouded Plain of Esdraelon. They were in a world alone, from which even the imposing Mount Tabor had disappeared into the clouds. The sun was slow to pierce the grayness, but when it did, the warming rays soon dispelled the mists and revealed the brownness of frost-tinged winter foliage. Gone were the bright blue flax and yellow mustard of spring. Only the green of the pine and cedar trees relieved the drabness.

At the Jordan River they came upon a camp of other Galileans journeying to census cities. The group gathered about the fire was filled with men who complained bitterly of the crowded inns along the way and of being forced to travel for the gathering of Roman taxes. Mary noticed that the mood of the travelers was entirely different than it was during the springtime journey. There were no other women travelers as only males were required to report to their native cities. These men were not traders from afar, they were farmers, shepherds, joiners, men of all trades. Even the merchants who were forced to travel were not bargaining and showing their wares as they had on Mary's first trip. Anger seethed beneath the attempted jovial chatter. Frequently Roman soldiers rode by on horses, rattling swords and armor, stopping now and then to question the assorted men. Mary and Joseph stayed to themselves.

In the rush to get the unpleasant journey over they all ate at dawn and did not pause until they stopped at dusk. Each rider carried hard cheese and bread to munch on plus a skin of wine to ease his thirst. The winter winds, full of sharp icy snow, stung their faces as the road climbed the mountains near Jericho. Mary was thankful for the heavy blanket which her father had sent along.

At noon on the fourth day part of the caravan turned off the road to Jerusalem and the remaining riders began the fifty furlongs to Bethlehem. Joseph and Mary could not keep up with the rapid pace of the men in the group and they lagged behind.

"I'm sorry, my husband, but I am unable to ride faster. Each step Jericho takes seems to jar me greatly and I am most uncomfortable."

"Do you want to stop here, Mary?" Joseph asked, "I will build a fire to keep the jackals at bay and I will stay awake while you rest."

"No, Joseph. My time is almost upon me. I know the child has dropped noticeably and I feel great pressure. If the scriptures are to be fulfilled we must get to Bethlehem with no delay."

"We will be late arriving. The sun is almost ready to set. There are so many people. I knew the city of David would be crowded, but I had no idea it would be like this. Perhaps we should have started sooner."

"I'm not worried," Mary stated firmly. " I know that Gabriel will be awaiting us with space reserved at the inn. The Lord God will want his child to be born in good surroundings. Probably this is all in the plan for us to travel here as our humble home would not be fitting for the birth of a king."

On foot, Joseph led Jericho over the rough places in the rocky road. He paused at the stone pillar beside the road at Ephrath.

"There is Rachel's tomb, Mary. Placed here by Jacob, who loved her as dearly as I love you." [1]

"Please help me down, my husband, so I may pray at the shrine of his great devotion." Mary knelt beside the stone. "*Boruch ato Adonai*," she said. "Thank you for blessing me with Joseph as you did Rachel with Jacob. I pray for your help within the next hours for I know my time is near. I am your servant, Lord, proud to do what I must do and I know no fear since I feel your nearness."

Joseph lifted her back onto Jericho. "It is only a short distance now. About seven more furlongs. We should be at the gate before closing time."

But Joseph was wrong. Darkness fell suddenly as it does in the lands of the mountains. When they reached the walls of Bethlehem, the gate had been closed. The travel-weary couple waited outside and was challenged by a guardsman.

Over the din of the crowd stirring inside, Joseph called out, "Can't you see, guardsman, that my wife is heavy in her travail? We must get to the inn and find a mid-wife. Her time is upon her."

Mary sat quietly, pale and suffering regular piercing pains. She clutched the heavy blanket about her and bit her lips to keep from crying out that she might not embarrass her husband. She told herself that it was only a matter of time until they would get to the inn where a room would be ready for her. She wondered if Gabriel would be in attendance. Surely he would be so that he might witness the Messiah's birth.

The guard and Joseph argued. Mary could not hear their words. As she looked about her everything seemed out of focus. Each flare divided into two, one yellow, one red. The leaves on the trees separated into blue and yellow. She felt faint, and wanted to lie down, but she remained on the ass, holding tightly to its head fearing she might fall.

Hurry! Hurry! Her mind raced with the streaks of pain. *Can't the guard see that I am ill? I must not faint and fall.* She saw Joseph give the man some coins and the gate opened slowly. With Joseph walking, leading the way, the little party moved in a single line.

The inn wasn't difficult to locate as it was surrounded by men who had come to the census-taking. Laughing wine-induced laughter, the few who had been in the caravan from Galilee had ceased complaining about the "unnecessary" travel. The journey had ended in a jubilee with much hugging and kissing of cheeks as distant cousins and uncles of the clan of David met together. They drank to David and to his descendants, one after another, until all were convinced the emperor had called the convocation for their enjoyment.

Again, Mary sat patiently while Joseph talked with the innkeeper who was busy pouring wine, laughing, yelling at his inn maids, trying to keep the noisy crowd satisfied. She saw the innkeeper shake his head. Then Joseph talked more, waving his hands about, pointing to Mary on Jericho. At last the man shrugged his shoulder, lifted his hands as if in despair, and pointed toward the side of the inn. He handed Joseph a flare.

Joseph hurried to Mary. "No arrangements were made, my wife. The inn is filled," he said.

"I can't believe that Gabriel did not have a room saved for me. After all . . . ." her voice trembled.

"The innkeeper said we may use the small stable in the cave behind the inn."

"A stable!" she cried out, unbelieving that this could be happening.

"It will be out of the weather. The man assured me there was plenty of fresh straw and hay for our animals, too."

"If that is the only place available we must go to the there at once. I must get off Jericho. My time is upon me."

Joseph found the path by the light of the flaming torch. Resigned to her fate Mary did not object and she urged Jericho to follow Jezreel. Even a pile of straw seemed a refuge from the torture of the long ride. The light flickered over the straw strewn stable. A cow, chewing her cud, turned her head and lowed at the interruption into the quiet cave. Three sheep came over, nosed about the intruders and then bleated their indignation. Joseph shooed them back and lifted Mary from her mount. He guided her to a corner, farthest from the stable-mates.

He tethered the two asses and began to remove soiled and soured straw from the area where Mary rested quietly. Relieved to be lying flat, her thoughts returned to the problem at hand.

"Did you ask the innkeeper where you could find a mid-wife to assist me?"

"I asked. He didn't know anyone but he promised to ask around to see if he could find such a woman."

"And if he finds no one?" Mary began to cry softly.

"I'll tend you, my little wife.

"That is forbidden. No man shall touch a woman at birthing. It is an unclean time."

"Nothing about you is unclean, Mary. If there is no one else, we will break the Law."

"Yes, yes. I will need someone strong to help me push or pull . . . whatever. My mother told me what to expect. Oh Joseph, I am afraid. I almost wish that I had stayed home. Mother always knows what to do. All the things she told me seem to have vanished from my mind with the regularity of the pains which are wracking me."

"How could the Lord let you down like this? Such an important event and no one here who knows what to do. I will be such a clumsy ox. Look at my hands. Calloused and rough. They are unfit to hold a babe."

"We must be practical, Joseph. We have to get the babe here before you can hold it. That is our biggest worry. First you must build a fire. We must warm water to bathe the child."

As Joseph began rolling some stones to confine a fire a sturdy woman looked into the stable and went to Mary.

"I saw you come into the courtyard on the ass. You seemed to be in the final throes of labor. I am a mid-wife," she said.

"I thank our Lord that you have come," Mary said. "What is your name?"

"You may call me Sarah."

"Joseph. Come meet Sarah. She is a mid-wife."

"Don't bother coming over here," the woman said in an authoritative voice. Joseph stopped as she barked out her orders. "Get that fire built so that the mother and babe will have a warm place and hot water. Bring plenty of fresh straw here. See that the animals stay at that end of the stable. And you stay out of my way. I've come to care for your wife. This is a time for women only."

The mid-wife loosened Mary's clothing and said, "You may cry out anytime you want to, and as loud as you need. No one will hear you."

"From what my mother told me, my time for crying out has not yet come. I know it will all be so much worse. I do not want to frighten my husband. When the time comes I cannot bear the pain, then I shall cry."

Mary felt a great a calm sweep over her. Her double color vision came into focus. This large woman reminded her of Joseph's mother before her illness had stripped her of her flesh. Even at her death her voice had remained strong and she directed her household with unfailing competency until the last week of her life. Mary thought, *If my mother-in-law were still alive she truly would have been my second mother.* Included in her reverie of memories of good days were the times with Elizabeth, the joy of being the Lord's handmaiden, her betrothal party, and her lovely wedding. She thought of her mother and Salome. Then her father and the boys visited her mind. She was riding again with the caravan family to Ein Karen. Little David asked if she would cry when she left him. She promised she would cry and she did.

A warmth spread over Mary. She detected a faint sweet odor of lilies. Even though she could not see him, she knew Gabriel was near, watching over her for the Lord. It had all been a part of the plan. The

Messiah was to be the Savior of all people so the birth was to take place in the lowliest shelter. Mary smiled and gave up her child with one great push.

"A perfect birth, my dear," the midwife said. "A beautiful son!"

Mary smiled and sank back on the straw bed, relieved that her ordeal had come to an end.

The woman, called Sarah, cleaned the tiny, wriggling, red-skinned body with warm water and rubbed him with the salt Mary had brought with her. Mary lifted her arms to receive her son. She inspected his head, his arms, his legs, and his torso to assure herself there was no flaw.

How irreverent of me, she thought. *As though God's child could have an imperfection.* She rejoiced in that perfection. She was delighted that he had inherited her own blonde hair and bright blue eyes.

"Sarah, please call my husband so that he might see our son's soundness," Mary said.

When Mary offered the baby, Joseph lifted him gently and cradled him in his muscular arm. Mary saw how fragile were the tiny legs and arms as they moved about on the large bronzed hands that knew rough timber better than they knew a child's delicate frame.

"Mary, our Jesus is perfect," he said.

"Jesus. That is a beautiful name," the midwife said. "A beautiful name for a beautiful baby."

Mary wrapped the child in the white swaddling cloths she had brought. Jericho moved from the far end of the stable to stand beside the mother and child as if to inspect the new resident. Joseph started to shoo her away when the cow, the sheep, and Jezreel came toward them also.

"Allow the animals to see our child for he shall love all creatures, both tame and wild, large or small. None shall run from him, nor he from them."

The little family, surrounded by the stable animals, did not notice when Sarah left. As suddenly as she appeared, she disappeared.

"We did not thank Sarah, nor pay her for her services. You must take some coins to the inn, plus this bright woolen scarf Elizabeth made for me. Hurry, she might still be there. If she is gone you can get directions where to find her."

Joseph piled fresh sweet scented hay in the manger near where Mary lay, and placed the child in it before he left. He returned very soon.

"The innkeeper did not know of such a woman. He said that evidently she saw you in the courtyard and sensed that you needed help. She must have followed us to the stable."

"How wonderfully strange," Mary said, but she knew who had come to help her. "*Boruch ato Adonai,*" she whispered.

Chapter Eighteen

The Star of Bethlehem Shines

Exhausted from the long journey and the birth, warm beneath Joachim's heavy blanket, Mary lay on the bed of fresh straw. She watched Joseph check the nearby manger where the baby lay and saw him lift a tiny hand, hold it, then tuck it beneath a soft woolen square.

Joseph tended the fire. In her drowsy state Mary was thankful that the stable was warmed against the bitter cold winds blowing off the mountains. She knew that she should thank the Lord for the safe comfort of her family, but her mind was too hazy to think of the right words. She saw that the oxen and the sheep had settled down in the far end of the cave stable. She watched Joseph mix grains for both Jericho and Jezreel.

Through the open door as Joseph stepped outside, Mary saw light, white and bright as sunshine. *Morning has come*, she thought. She was not surprised that the night watch hours had sped away unnoticed. So much had happened. Yet she felt confused. There were no blushing streaks announcing the rising sun.

"Has dawn come already?" Mary asked, drawling sleep-tinged words. "I am so tired, and yet I cannot sleep."

Joseph looked up. "No, it is not morning," he said. "From directly over this stable, light is coming from a star, blazing like a fire-brand. I don't recall such a star when we came in."

"It was very dark then, Joseph. Remember how thankful we were for the torch the innkeeper gave you?"

"Do you hear soft voices singing or am I just imagining them?"

"Yes, Joseph, I do. In the distance. Like a choir."

The muted music came nearer. The sound came from above and Mary heard voices singing, "Glory to God in the highest, and on earth peace, good will toward men." [1]

She closed her eyes to pray when she heard feet shuffling outside. She sat up and listened to the voices of men approaching the stable. There was no scuffling, no loud shouts, no threats. Still, her heart beat faster not knowing what danger might be threatening her child. Immediately she reached for the baby and held him tightly in her arms.

Joseph opened the door and said to those outside, "Come into the stable and warm yourselves. It is a very cold night and I have a good fire within."

With woolen head-scarves and heavy, fleece-lined cloaks glistening with drops of melted snow, three shepherds followed Joseph. As they entered, all bowed deep, extending their hands at the knee. The eldest stepped forward. His face was leather-brown and wrinkled, his hair white, and his back bent double from years of laboring in all weathers. He said in a halting, hoarse voice,

"We were tending our flocks of the temple sheep, resting on the hillside, when we heard singing but we couldn't see anyone. Then we looked up and saw a band of what appeared to be angels, shining bright as day. One came down and stood right there before us. We were sore afraid. Not knowing how to act before an angel, we fell down and put our heads to the ground.

"The angel said for us not to be afraid for they brought good news and great joy to everyone. They said that Christ, who would be our Savior was born this day in the city of David. Then they said that for a sign to us we would find a baby wrapped in swaddling cloths, lying in a manger. [1]

"Well, all the angels began singing again, sounded like 'Glory to God in the highest' and flew away. Then Taddy here, we call him Taddy, but his real name is Thaddaeus," he placed his hand on a boy's shoulder, "Well, Taddy saw a real bright star move and then stop and we figured it stopped around somewhere in Bethlehem. We were curious and came here where it shined the brightest."

Joseph smiled. "You are the baby's first visitors," he said as he stepped forward and motioned for the three to follow.

"Mary, it seems these shepherds were shown the way to the stable by the angels you heard singing."

"And the star!" the lad Taddy said. His clothes were soiled and ragged, his face dirty, but the smile reflected his pride for having been the first to see the star.

"Where is this Savior?" the tall muscular man of about twenty years said. In one hand he held a shepherd's staff. The other hand he placed on his hip, and looked about the stable as if he were in doubt that the men were in the right place.

"In his mother's arms," Joseph said proudly. Mary lifted the swaddled child so that all might see him.

"But he's so little," Taddy said. "My father told me we would have a Messiah come to lead us into a victory against the Romans. But this is only a baby!"

Mary answered him softly, "But a very special baby, Thaddaeus. I do not know by what means our Lord plans to save Israel. All I know is that this child is the Son of God."

"We will remember this night," the old man said, nodding his head as he pulled at his white beard. He put his weathered hand on the boy's shoulder, "You, especially, my lad. I am an old man, with few years left, but you have many years to live. You will remember you saw the Messiah and can tell your children."

"Who will believe three shepherds?" the tall one said as he looked from the mother and baby, to the two poorly dressed creatures beside him. "No one! Angels don't come down to people like us and tell them where to go to find the Messiah! That's hard for even me to believe . . . and yet I guess I do. I know what I saw and what I heard. I won't ever forget all those angels . . . it has to be true." He knelt beside the manger and at his feet he lay his staff with URIA carved on the crook. "I have nothing to give that the babe might use, but perhaps it may be useful to you, his earthly father, as you protect him during your travels."

The old man pulled a shepherd's scrip bag from the depths of his heavy sheep hide cloak. "Give him this," he said as he placed the freshly dressed skin of a kid, already finished into a carrying bag. "This will be good to carry his things in."

Thaddaeus said, "I'm sorry I haven't anything at all for the baby's gift." He held his head down, and twisted the tattered robe that he had held together with tight fists all the while.

"What about that shepherd's pipe I made for you today, my little brother?" the tall man asked.

The boy's face spread a wide smile. "Do you think he'd like that? He's very little to play a pipe." He hurriedly placed the new pipe on top of the bag. "But he'll grow. What is the baby's name?"

"Jesus," Mary answered.

"That pipe plays real sweet notes, Jesus, and when you get older I hope you'll like to make music, just like I do."

The old man started toward the door. "We'd better hurry back to our flocks," he said. "There's jackals and wild dogs just waiting for a chance to get those fat temple sheep."

Mary thanked them for coming. She knew that the gifts had been important to each one and she accepted them graciously.

The shepherds left and the angel music continued but it was soon interrupted by a man's voice full of alarm shouting outside the door, "What's going on in there?"

Joseph hurried to the door and opened it slightly, then pulled it wider as he said, "It's the innkeeper. Come in, sire."

A rotund man, with a wide cloth stained red with wine tied about his full girth, swept in and pushed Joseph aside.

"Something is going on in here and I want to know what it is," he said. "First light from a star, then voices singing from nowhere, and now three shepherds going out into the courtyard shouting 'Long live the Messiah!' The drunken gentiles out there may not know what a messiah is, but I am of the house of David as are many of my guests. We know what that means and I can't afford to be a party to anything like proclaiming a false Messiah. We have had enough of that. One messiah after another. Riot after riot. I am a poor innkeeper trying to make a living for my family and I can't have rabble rousers shouting things that might be taken as against Herod or the Romans. A man has to do what he has to do to appease all the officials. You understand what I mean?"

"We are not here to cause trouble, sire. Come see for yourself," Joseph said as he motioned toward the manger where Mary and the baby lay. "He was born just hours ago."

"You told me that your wife was about to have a baby. But the Messiah! I don't believe you. Our Lord has promised us a leader and we all know we are looking for a royal descendent of David to lead us."

Mary said softly, "It was difficult for me to understand why we were chosen but indeed we are of David's stock. This child has been delivered to fulfill the Holy Scripture."

"Don't you recall the prophecy that a child would born to a virgin here in Bethlehem?" Joseph asked.

"The Lord would not allow the Messiah to be . . . ," the man lifted his hands in despair. "I don't understand. Those shepherds . . . how did they know?"

"The shepherds were watching their sheep when they heard the angels and followed the light of the star to your inn."

"This is almost too much to believe . . . yet I did hear the angels sing and saw the star. If it is so . . . oh . . . to think I sent you to the stable to have the Messiah in with the animals." He lifted his hands higher and looked upward. "*Boruch ato Adonai* forgive me. Forgive me for not knowing."

"There is nothing to forgive. We are quite comfortable. Come see our Jesus," Mary said.

The innkeeper knelt down. "My Lady," he said, "I will tell no one of this meeting but it will be in my heart always. No one will believe that the Messiah was born in my stable. I will be persecuted by some who will blame me for mistreating the Messiah's mother, others will blame me for allowing him to be born on my grounds. In these days, silence is the only safe path. There are spies and enemies at every threshold. You understand?"

"Of course, " Mary smiled. "But *Adonai* will never forget you. You took us in when we needed room. It is all a part of a plan. "

"You may stay here as long as you like. When I have a room vacant I shall move you . . . ."

"No, this stable is fine. My husband is a fine carpenter and he will be able to fix this up into a pleasant place for us until we take our son to be redeemed at the Temple."

"You shall stay here as long as you need," the innkeeper said. "My name is Shammah, named for one of David's older brothers. But for a twist in fate, Shammah would have been named king by Samuel instead of David."

"That is past history now, Shammah," Joseph said. "Tonight we are looking to the future of Israel."

"True, and perhaps with your son it will come to pass. I will see you tomorrow at the inn," he shrugged his shoulders and then nodded his farewell as he backed out the door and closed it behind him.

With the quiet came the soft singing again. Mary looked at the baby and said, "When you are old enough we will tell you of this night. Oh Joseph, this night may be the most important night in all Israel."

Then Joseph told Mary how he had felt when he lifted the tiny baby fingers as he covered the sleeping child. "I marveled at the new creation. I'd seen babies many times but I had never held one, or examined the delicately formed hand of a newborn. I'm not sure what I expected of this child, this Son of God. Man was created in God's image, so the Torah says. But I have wondered all these months if this was an experiment, this mixing of a human with the Holy Spirit.

"I've heard that Romans and Greeks have many half-gods. They have gods for every phase of life. Then I reasoned that our one God, *Adonai*, would not give our people a half-god son. He had promised Israel a Messiah—a Redeemer—a Savior. No half-god could be that. I worry how this infant, dependent upon us—mere human parents, could lead our land to freedom from the crushing rule of the Caesars and the Herods of the world."

"It is a frightening thought, my husband. I have held this worry in my heart for all these months, too. I've wondered what I was bearing. I've wondered what he would look like . . . would he be ethereal like an angel with no substance but a glowing frame? Perhaps like Gabriel? Or would he have a fearsome face which would frighten people into submission? Oh, I have lain awake many nights trying to figure all this out, but I found no answers, Joseph, when I saw this precious baby, frail and perfect. I knew everything would be all right. The Lord entrusted us to be good parents. Jesus will grow up and he will know what his Father, our one God, expects of him. We have no choice, Joseph. We have no choice but to love him as we would any sweet baby. Whatever is to be special about this child will become known to us at the proper time."

Chapter Nineteen

The Circumcision of Jesus

The night was short. After the visitors left, Mary and Joseph marveled at the visitations. If there had been any doubts about the child's holy status, they were dispelled with the angel chorus, the brilliant star, and, the worshiping shepherds. With dawn came the blush-streaked sky and the education of the new parents that an infant, even a holy one, demands attention. Jesus cried, as any baby cries: to be fed, to go to sleep, and to be changed. Mary felt a deep surge of motherhood when, for the first time, the small mouth sought her breast as greedily as any newborn animal seeks its food source. Finding its goal, the mouth did not know how to suck. Jesus burrowed, nuzzled and pursed his lips. With the first drop of milk Mary shared his success.

With the baby cradled in her arm, Mary discreetly covered her breast with her robe and proudly performed her important motherhood role as Joseph watched. He laughed at the noisy, smacking sound and the waving hands that reminded him of a baby-bird's wing-fluttering while it is being fed. When Jesus fell asleep, his hunger pangs satisfied, Joseph took him from Mary's arms and held him close to his shoulder as she directed.

"How do you know so much?" Joseph asked.

"I watched my mother and I was old enough to hold both of my brothers."

"I don't think I'll ever feel at ease holding him," Joseph said. "He's so tiny I'm afraid he'll break."

"I assure you—he won't," Mary laughed. "Newborns are stronger than you think."

At the sixth hour a maid, from the inn, brought them a noontime lunch of cheese, dates, and warm bread which filled the stable with a rich aroma.

"How neighborly of the innkeeper. How did he know that I was hungry when I had never thought of eating?" Mary laughed as she tore off a piece of the thick, golden crust to eat with some cheese. "This really makes me feel at home. Joseph, I have been so happy to have you and the baby here with me in this warm and cozy place."

"Perhaps Gabriel is watching out for you. After we have eaten I want you to rest, my wife. You have had a tiring journey and our child is quiet now." Mary noticed the word "our." She wanted to hug Joseph in her moment of happiness, but she made no mention and listened as he went on. "Try to get some sleep. I will stop by the inn to thank Shammah for his kindness, then I must go pay my dues to Caesar. The guard let us in after the collector had left his post for the night. I promised to return early today. Then I thought I might move about and inquire if any of my brothers are in Bethlehem."

"That would be a pleasant surprise. Do bring them back with you if you find them. And I promise to rest."

"Would that you might let me hold you close, Mary. I feel a great need of you now. "

"I feel the need, too, but I am unclean, Joseph. You must not touch my person, my clothing, sit nor lie upon my bed, or even sit in a chair I have been on, until I am ritually cleansed, you know that!"

"Unclean! Totally ridiculous to say that of you, my wife."

"It is so written. Moses gave us the Law."

"Well, I know. For forty days!"

Mary laughed. "We're lucky he wasn't a girl. Then we'd have to wait eighty days."

"True," Joseph said over his shoulder as he went out the door,

Time moved at a snail's pace for Mary. The baby slept soundly in his manger crib. Tired and feeling very alone Mary dozed and awakened often while Joseph was gone. She was startled and fully awakened by the rasping sound of the crude door scraping over the stone floor when Joseph returned. She greeted him joyously.

"Back already?" *Already! It had been an eternity!* "Did you find any of your family?"

"They had all been here several days ago, registered and left. None of them had to come as far as we did."

"I'd hope to show them little Jesus." She looked into the manger at her side. "I will be up and about tomorrow. I need to wash things we soiled on our trip here." She noticed Joseph was walking about, testing a board here and there, measuring spaces with his outstretched arms. "What are you doing?" she asked.

"I think I can make this stable into a pleasant place to stay. The weather has warmed a lot. Sharp winds have calmed and slowly the sun is warming the streets and tile roofs. Already there seems a touch of newness in the air. I talked with the innkeeper and he was agreeable to my trading work for our lodging and some food. He's really a very pleasant man.

"He apologized for his actions last evening. He said he was very tired and worried about trouble for his inn. Everyone here seems nervous and upset about the yoke of taxes that have been put upon all of us . . . plus the cruelty of foreign rulers and soldiers. Being so close to Jerusalem they see more of the terror of Herod's reign and the chicanery of the Roman puppets, as well as the conflict between the Pharisees and the Sadducees, than we know in Galilee."

That evening Shammah's wife, Esther, brought a steaming pot of lamb and barley potage to the stable. "I thought you might not feel up to cooking so soon after having a child," she said. "I know how it is. I had seven children . . . five of them boys. All grown now but I have many grandchildren about me most of the time."

Esther looks like a grandmother should, Mary thought. She was short with an ample figure, and laugh wrinkles about her eyes and mouth. She wore her gray hair in a knot at the nape of her neck which reminded Mary of her own mother. How could seeing hair coiled in a certain way reinforce the distance between Bethlehem and Nazareth? She missed her mother and father.

The woman's voice cut into Mary' s moment of homesickness. "I know you are very far from home and your family. My husband told me that you wished to stay to take the child into the Temple for his redemption. But what of his circumcision? Since you are alone in Bethlehem, I assume you have not yet made any plans for that. Shammah and I would be proud to be stand-in grandparents."

"Oh yes," Mary almost cried out. "Oh yes. I have been missing my parents so much. And I have been thinking about the naming ceremony. I remember so well about my brothers. We had a lovely party for each of them. Of course there were many relatives around us to share that important day when a boy is officially marked as a child of our Lord."

"Then we shall plan to have a lovely party for your son, too."

After Esther left, Mary lay thinking about all that had happened to her in that one day. Somehow she could not think of herself as a mother, yet she knew that her relationship with her son was the same as her mother's to her. The first born. The close tie between a mother and her first born. Perhaps it was the newness of the relationship of one body creating another; the remembrance of the first time the baby stirred within her and the months of feeling the thrusting of a tiny foot or hand seeking freedom from the tight enclosure of her body. Perhaps it was the nursing, the nurturing of a totally dependent creature that created the tie.

Upon their arrival the night before and finding no room reserved in the inn, Mary felt that Gabriel should have made plans for them. Now she knew that he had. When Joseph heard of Esther's visit, he agreed with Mary their stay in the inn's stable was no accident or oversight by *Adonai*.

And so it came about that in the early morning, on the eighth day after his birth, Mary and Joseph took Jesus to the owner's living quarters at the inn. Taking the traditional place that would have been Grandfather Joachim's, Shammah was to be the sandak to hold Jesus on the white linen pillow, which Mary had made for the ceremony. Mary wanted to be present but Joseph said that it was not pleasant for a mother to watch her child being cut.

Standing just beyond the door, she heard Joseph recite the commandment of the covenant with Abraham. Shammah offered the blessing for wine and all went well until Mary heard the baby's shrill cry. She wanted to rush in to comfort him, but she restrained herself out of respect for Joseph's wishes and remained away from the room until it was proper for her to appear. Jesus was quiet by the time Joseph motioned for her to come join them. She took her son in her arms and wiped a tiny drop of red wine from his rosebud mouth.

"According to the laws of Moses, the first born is dedicated to our Lord. We do so dedicate our child, Jesus," Joseph said.

"He was dedicated to our Lord from the moment I knew of him," Mary said. "Each day from that day forward I have never neglected dedicating him to the service of our Lord, whatever that service might be."

As though they were members of her family, Esther had prepared a feast in honor of this important event. No one mentioned the Messiah, the star, or the angels. Their host had kept his word not to broadcast that news. As guests he had invited all neighbors, as well the help at the inn. Since it was too early in the day for travelers, there were none there seeking shelter for the night.

This was the day that the Lord's Son was officially named. From this day forward he would be marked a Jew, a true son of Israel. Before sundown, Shammah and Joseph buried the small package of white linen which held the severed foreskin, so that it might become a part of the land of Israel forever.

Toward the end of the month a red sunset promised spring-like weather. On the morning of the thirtieth day after the birth, the sun leaped into the sky to warm the little family traveling to Jerusalem. Mary, carrying the baby wrapped in a white wool blanket, rode on Jericho. Joseph walked ahead proudly holding the gift staff, with the carving URIA in his left hand and clasping Jericho's red leather, gaily-decorated halter with his right one. The importance of the journey rode with them for this was the day Jesus was to be redeemed at the Temple.

The sun pierced the clouds with ladders of light, dancing spots over the red-tinged rocks and green tree tops in the distance. The lingering, crisp, night air wafted into thin mists as the sun warmed the red, roof tiles. The paved road, skimming the crest of the mountains, was crowded with moving people: farmers going to sell grain or vegetables, shepherds with animals to market, merchant craftsmen and their wares, plus many worshipers going to the Temple. Even the boisterous rabble of the inn-courtyard seemed quiet to the jostling crowds nearing the city. Vendors called out to attract attention: the more daring ones rushed to tug at Mary's skirt or to pluck at Joseph's sleeve. Loud laughter came from groups huddled along the way where men slapped each other's shoulders while tale swapping.

The road passed beside Herod's palace, with its three tall towers to remind all viewers that they were passing the residence of Herod with its Great High walls with posted guards. Through a gate, slightly ajar, Mary saw the cultivated flower beds that were in the inner compound. Passing through the Garden Gate, where the roads from Bethlehem and Joppa joined to enter the city of Jerusalem, a steady stream flowed like a river into a street tightly packed with people, donkeys, and camels wending down the narrow lane toward the Temple. Expectancy rode with the crowd. Mary could not deny the excitement which filled her as she came into the city for the first time as an adult. Years before she had been there but it didn't seem the same.

Sometimes the sun dipped down to light the deeply-shadowed, narrow, booth-lined streets named for the articles or services offered for sale. Such descriptive names as Silversmith, Bread, and Fish directed shoppers to the proper markets. Vegetable Street amazed Mary with its colorful piles of assorted melons, artichokes, and other foreign foods which were unknown to her. Joseph, with his wooden chip anchored firmly over his ear, melted into this crowd of assorted workmen: dyers with colored rags and scribes with pens perched over ears, or tailors sporting shiny needles on their robe shoulders. Bedouins in brightly striped robes, leading over-loaded camels, slowed the steady parade. A fat silk-robed man, with every finger ringed with gold, reminded Mary of Benjamin.

Narrow lanes branched off into a vast labyrinth of houses and shops where old men in dark robes, with prayer shawls over their heads, rocked back and forth, chanting prayers in monotonous tones. Young boys stood beside them imitating their actions. The confusion increased as they came nearer to the Temple. At last it came into full view, with its marble and gold glistening in the bright sunshine. Mary saw the golden eagle spreading its wings over the portico.

"Why is there an eagle on God's House?" she asked.

"Herod appeases Caesar with a Roman emblem," Joseph answered. "I suppose we must be thankful for his rebuilding the Temple for us after all the years of the destruction of a holy place for our Lord."

"Don't the priests or the Sanhedrin object?"

"I think they feel that since the Lord has not struck it with lightening, that perhaps He feels the eagle is His bird also. It is not wise to twist a lion's tail."

"Joseph, all these people selling animals and grain and trading money make me feel ill. The stench of animal dung, plus the pall of sacrificial smoke from burnt offerings . . . the noise of the vendors hawking to get attention is deafening plus the pitiful calls of animals and the incessant chatter of people. Who can worship in this confusion?"

"Only in this Court of Gentiles do you find confusion. When we enter the Temple proper it will be different. You'll see."

"The odor and the cries of the animals will still be there."

"To the Lord the odor of burnt sacrifice is holy. Now we must find a boy who seems honest to look after Jericho while we are in the temple. I will give him a coin when we return."

"Isn't that Thaddaeus, the shepherd boy, standing on the steps?"

Taddy saw them and came running. "I brought lambs in for the morning sacrifices," he said.

"We are looking for a boy to watch our ass while we take the baby in to be redeemed. Do you know one?" Joseph asked.

His face beamed. "I will be pleased to watch her for you. It would be an honor to care for the animal who carries our Messiah."

Turbaned heads turned, shoulders shrugged at the word Messiah. The crowd pushed on into the Temple. Joseph went to a table of a money-changer to get the five shekels he would need to hand the priest during the ceremony. Mary stopped as she noticed the words carved in the stone above the entry way and asked,

"I cannot read Greek, Joseph. Do you know what the sign says?"

"I can't read Greek either but I know what it says: Let no alien pass through the barrier about the sanctuary. Anyone so trespassing will pay with his life." [2]

"Surely those are not the words of our One God, are they, Joseph?"

"He has said no one shall look upon His face. Perhaps the high priests decided that no alien should be allowed to break the Law which we Jews must honor."

"But to pay with a life seems to be a harsh penalty for entering anyplace," Mary said. "Especially if one cannot read the warning."

"Come now, my Wife. We cannot change the Temple to suit your ideas of fairness. There are some things in life we have to accept. The Laws of Moses have ruled our people for centuries, and no doubt will rule them for many more. Do not worry your pretty head about something you can do nothing about.

"Perhaps, in time, when our son is declared king, he will make changes in the Temple. Until then . . . let us go about dedicating him to the service of our one God."

As the little family started toward the Inner Court they were approached by an old man whose squinting black eyes glittered in a wrinkled, parchment face. About his shoulders, he clutched a worn prayer shawl with the thick, yellowed finger-nails of his shriveled hands. He moved slowly and his body shook with age-tremors. He looked up and smiled as he came toward Mary, who was carrying the baby.

"May I hold him a moment?" he asked in a trembling, weak voice.

"Of course," Mary said as she carefully transferred her white robed child to his arms. She was pleased to have her beautiful son admired.

Rocking back and forth, with his rheumy eyes uplifted, the old man chanted,

"Lord, now lettest thou thy servant depart in peace, according to thy word; For mine eyes have seen thy salvation which thou has prepared in the presence of all peoples, A light for revelation to the Gentiles and for glory to thy people Israel." [1]

"How nice of you to bless our son." Mary said smiling and taking Jesus from the quivering, old arms.

"Behold, this child is set for the fall and rising of many in Israel," the old man said. "And for a sign that is spoken against (and a sword will pierce through your own soul also), that thoughts out of many hearts may be revealed." [3]

Mary held the baby tightly against her breast, then bewildered, she looked up to Joseph. *What does he mean, a sword?* she wondered, but she did not ask aloud.

"Simeon is my name," the old man went on. "I've waited patiently all the years of my life for this moment. I am ready to die now."

A white haired woman leaning hard against a staff, hobbled to the old man's side. She clasped her small clawlike hands together and prayed,

"Thanks be to the Lord." Tears streamed from her pale eyes as the man, who called himself Simeon, took her arm.

"Come, Prophetess Anna," he said. "Our days of waiting and praying are over. We have seen the Messiah. So it has been written that we may depart this world now, knowing that we have been blest as we had hoped." The two tottered away and became a part of the gathering crowd.

Joseph took Jesus from Mary's arms so that he might join the men in the Inner Court, while she remained in the Court of Women with other wives and mothers awaiting ceremonial sacrifices.

Chapter Twenty

Mary s Cleansing Rites

In the late afternoon on the fortieth day of living in Bethlehem, Joseph, Mary, and Jesus went to Jerusalem for the final birth ritual, the Purification of the Mother. The road was filled with travelers, some returning from a day at the market buying or selling, others going to find shelter in the city. Already torches were being lit along the way, making a stream of lights moving to and from the city.

Again they went past Herod's palace and through the Garden Gate to mingle with the stream of people, camels, and asses. They wound their way through vendors hawking their wares of colorful vegetables, exotic fruits, fresh-caught fish, bleating lambs, and goats. The cacophony of sight and sound and smell enthralled Mary. If the city impressed Joseph he made no sign for he was busy threading a pathway for his family.

The distant sight of the white marble Temple, burnished gold by the late sun, spurred Joseph to hurry Jericho's slow pace. As the westerly mountains plunged into deep shadows, the Temple glowed with flaming torches set about the thirty broad steps leading up to the Royal Portico. Joseph tied Jericho to a post at the base of the steps and the little family went up and entered the Court of Gentiles. An air of solemn mystery enveloped the massive building now void of the pressing crowds of worshipers, money changers, and livestock. The corridor leading to the mikvah was lined with flickering oil lamps splattering eerie light patterns into the darkness.

Mary hesitated at the stairway leading to the pool. Immediately she was joined by a white gowned woman who said, in a kindly voice, as she appeared at a dark doorway,

"Come this way, my dear."

Mary looked up to Joseph.

"Don't be afraid," he said. "I'll be waiting for you right here."

"I am not afraid. This is the Lord's house. I have no need of fear . . . except . . . I've never been here before and I don't know where I should go."

"That lady, the keeper of the baths, will show you."

Mary exchanged the baby in her arms for the bundle of her clean clothes, which Joseph had been carrying. She looked down into the stairwell and saw, at the bottom, the pool of water with light reflections dancing over its slightly, rippling surface.

"Be careful on the steps, my dear," the woman attendant called. "Bring a light with you."

Mary took a torch from a holder and went down to the pool's edge. As the attendant took the bundle of clean clothing she motioned toward a nearby small room. Mary undressed. She wondered if the woman would be there when she came out, naked, to enter the pool. She hoped not. Not once had she been seen or seen another unclothed person, not even when she and her mother went to the stream together to be purified after they had cared for Rebecca's body. One had bathed while the other watched for intruders. Her mother had ceased attending her bath when she had learned to care for herself, except that one time on her wedding day. She would never forget the humiliation of that experience.

She was relieved to find the pool area empty as she stepped over the cold stone floor and went down steps, one at a time, until she reached the full depth of the chilled water. She immersed herself completely, according to the way her mother had taught her, spreading her legs and arms, even her fingers, to be certain that the water would touch every inch of her body. She prayed the prayers of purification to *Adonai*, feeling his presence in the enfolding waters.

After the third immersion she walked up the steps on the opposite side of the mikvah and found a clean cloth hanging beside the top step. Quickly she wrapped it around her, and the woman appeared saying, "Your clean clothes are in there. I have your unclean things wrapped, ready for you to take with you."

Wearing a fresh blue robe, with her long hair still damp, Mary went up to Joseph and said, "I know that *Adonai* heard my prayers of thanksgiving for the privilege of being the mother of His Son. It was as if He were there with me. The cold waters became warm and I felt His loving arms about me. Oh, Joseph, it was like the miracle all over again."

Mary and Joseph walked past the place where Simeon and the Prophetess Anna had stopped them on the day Jesus had been redeemed. Mary reminded Joseph of the meeting.

"Do you think that will happen all the time—people knowing?" she asked.

"No. When we get back to Nazareth and home, people will accept Jesus as an ordinary child." Joseph said as they walked along the long corridor.

"Tomorrow we will be starting back to Nazareth, Joseph. I will be happy to be back in our own home . . . and to see my family. I miss every one of then. I want to show our beautiful child, of course. But, this has been a wondrous time for me. The baby is so dear and you have been with me almost every minute."

"And I haven't been earning much either. That is not good for a man with a new family," Joseph laughed. "But I'll make up for lost time when we do get home."

"My only sorrow is that I did not get to see Elizabeth and little John."

"I asked around the market place yesterday and found out a little about the Essenes. They don't call themselves that. Could be why no one seemed to know who I was asking about. They go by many names, such as, 'the brethren', 'they that believe', 'the poor', and a few more. There seem to be groups all over Judea. They maintain a monastery at Qumran where Elizabeth said she would be living."

"Oh, I do wish that I could see her," Mary said.

"'Qumran is on the west bank of the Great Salt Lake. We could make a side trip on the way home. There is a road from Jerusalem, over the Mount of Olives. "

"Could we? Would you do that for me, Joseph?"

"I would do anything to make you happy, Mary. You know that. But I don't think you will like it there. Everyone says that the people are fanatics. They don't agree with either the Pharisees or the Sadducees. They claim to live by the religion of Moses, as he gave it, without interpretations by priests or scribes."

"Elizabeth's letter said they are very kind and that they believe in the coming Messiah. They believe that little John will be a prophet to pave the way for Him. When Elizabeth tells them of Jesus' miraculous birth they will acknowledge him to be the Savior. I know they will. I almost feel compelled to go, Joseph."

That night they camped along with many other travelers and worshipers in the garden at the foot of the Mount of Olives. They could see the lighted lamps around the Temple glowing throughout the night.

At the first stab of pink light, the clarion call of the shofar drifted from the Temple roof. Already smoke curled from the fires being readied for the day's sacrifices. The campers arose and joined the throng waiting for the call to worship.

By the time Mary had fed Jesus, a crowd had gathered in the Court of the Gentiles. Joseph went to one of the many tables where worshipers exchanged Roman denarii into shekels needed to purchase sacrifices. The turbaned man did not look up as he fingered and stacked the piles of money before him. Mary was repulsed by the grimy hands that counted the coins into Joseph's hand. There were many "Gifts for *Adonai*" available to place upon the holy altar: expensive incense, newborn lambs, oxen as well as delicate white pigeons and doves. Mary chose two white doves. She shuddered at the rough handling of the birds, which were to be offered for her cleansing. The birds fluttered and struggled to be free until Mary smoothed their soft white feathers and held them close to her cheeks.

"I really can't understand why our Lord demands these beautiful creatures to be killed for a sacrifice," Mary said.

"We're not the ones to question what the Lord wants. We must follow the law in the Torah," Joseph reminded her.

"But that was written such a long time ago. Surely *Adonai* knows that His animals are being mistreated. Surely He hears their cries."

"Mary, we have no choice. Come, it is time for you to present the sacrifice to the priests for your purification. Let us go into the Court of Women now. "

Joseph gave Mary the coins required and she dropped them in one of the tall flared vases on either side of the steps leading to the sacred area. No woman was allowed to enter where the priests presided over the sacrificial altar. For once Mary did not resent the denial to a service: she was glad that she could not see the bloodletting, or the fluttering wings of the white birds. After all the ceremonies were over, Joseph and Mary walked around the Temple to the tall gate looking eastward.

Joseph said, "This is called the Beautiful Gate. It is made of polished brass, and they say it is so heavy it takes twenty men to open and close it, although I've never been here when that was done."

"It is well named with its delicate scroll work. *Adonai* must love looking out over his land from this point. Just look at the mountains sloping up to the deep blue, cloudless sky."

"We are facing the east. That is the Mount of Olives. The road over it leads to the Salt Sea."

"You mean that is the road to Qumran? The one we will take when we go to see Elizabeth?"

"It seems the best way. The road won't be too busy, not many care to go down the depths of that hot, dry valley. It is steep and dangerous. Few have need to go as there are no fish in the water. Too salty."

"Why are there so many little paths scattered over the hill?"

"Paths to the sepulchers. Right now they are all weathered but come Passover the stones will be whitened so that they will shine out in the Pascal moon."

"That must look quite eerie. The thought of tombs depress me. Depression has lain heavy upon me since that old man warned about the sword piercing through my soul—and that our child is set for the fall and rising of many in Israel. What did he mean, Joseph?"

"I don't know. He seemed to be quite happy to accept Jesus as the Messiah. He never questioned that a moment. Was he telling us that nurturing a Messiah may not be easy but will be full of anguish for you, his mother?"

"I thought that is what he meant. I have prepared myself for a future that will not be easy. Since Jesus has been sent to save Israel he has much to learn, We must find good rabbis to teach him. Oh Joseph, it will be exciting to study with him."

"Most of that will be your task, my wife. I shall have to make a living to keep us fed and clothed. But I would that you not think of the old man's words. He recognized Jesus as the Messiah! That is the miracle!"

"And old Anna. What proof! As if we needed any to know the truth."

Taking her arm to turn her from the gate toward the street leading to the Bethlehem Road, Joseph said, "We should leave early in the morning so we will have time to look for your cousin as those people live in caves in the hillside. I understand they have a monastery to prepare young girls to be the chosen virgin mother of the Messiah."

"Somehow those people will know that I am that virgin and their search is over. I have no doubt we will find Elizabeth, Joseph. The Lord will lead us, as He has all the way."

Chapter Twenty-one

The Three Magi Find Jesus

The inn was beginning to fill with travelers when the little family made its way toward the quiet cave-stable, which had become their friendly home.

While Mary folded their garments, Joseph went to tell the innkeeper that they would be leaving early in the morning. Shammah, his wife Esther, and the workers at the inn had been generous with the young couple during their stay: the innkeeper gave them their "home" rent-free and praised Joseph for the carpentry work he had done; Esther visited with Mary as they sewed and embroidered together; and the women workers often brought sweetmeats and fruits to the neat stable home. No one spoke of Jesus as the Messiah, but he lacked nothing in adoration as a sweet and beautiful baby. This pleased the new mother.

It was late afternoon when Shammah brought a steaming pot of lamb and vegetable stew and Esther carried a honey cake. "A going away dinner," Shammah said as he placed the pot on the table.

"A celebration dinner honoring all the ceremonies we've attended lately," Mary said joyfully.

"We wish you a good journey home. God be with you. Do stop in to see us whenever you are traveling this way."

"Thank you so much. You've been like parents to us," Mary hugged each one.

"We shall miss you," Joseph said as he was closing the door.

The two enjoyed a happy meal with good food and the promise of seeing friends and relatives in Nazareth once again. When they finished dining, Joseph began packing the panniers for Jezreel's pack. Mary straightened the living area, and said her goodbyes to the animals who had patiently shared their home for forty days.

The sun set, darkness deepened. Mary lit flickering oil lamps to brighten the stable while Joseph returned the empty dinner pot to the inn. As Mary placed the baby's supplies in his new scrip the shepherd had given him, she heard men talking and camels snorting. She recalled when she rode in a caravan for the first time, how camels' raucous cries had frightened her, but now she had become accustomed to hearing them and they didn't upset her any more. She went on packing, and thrust the shepherd's whistle deep in the packet.

Joseph pushed aside the door easily. It no longer grated along the rough stone floor as it had that first night. Joseph had repaired it as he remade the stable. A brilliant light flooded into the dim stable and Mary turned to see its source.

"My wife," Joseph said, "these men are magi from Chaldea." [1]

Standing in front of the manger, Mary tried to hide the baby as the three men with sun-parched faces swept into the room. To her they were threateningly tall and large beside Joseph, and then, she realized that it was their clothing which made then appear oversized. They wore high, tightly twisted turbans, and long sweeping silk robes which flowed from their shoulders as they walked. Each held a box with both hands.

In unison they said, "We have come to see the new King of the Jews." [1]

"The king?" Mary asked timidly, fearful that these colorfully garbed men might be bent on harming her child.

"The Messiah that was foretold to be born in Bethlehem of Judea."

"The Messiah," Mary sighed. "Then you mean him no harm." She took Jesus up in her arms and showed him.

The man with a flowing, white beard stepped forward. He was dressed in a black, corded-silk robe with silver chains and amulets. On his head a band of glittering jewels circled a tall black and white turban.

"My name is Balthazar," he said. "We three have been studying the conjunction of the planets Jupiter, Saturn, and Mars which occurs with a brilliant display only once every 794 years. We have concluded that this should be the sign of the ruler of the last days. We followed its bright light from our land to Judea then suddenly we lost sight of it. Since we sought a new King of the Jews we naturally stopped at King Herod's court to see the royal prince. But no one there knew of a royal birth."

The second man, dressed in red silk, richly embroidered in gold, stepped out. About his neck hung gold chains ending in a large disc, glistening with radiating sun-rays. Above his sand-colored hair and neatly-clipped beard was a red and gold turban, tightly rolled to a peak. He bowed low before he spoke in a soft voice.

"I am Gaspar, also of Chaldea. We have come to pay homage to the new born King. Little did we think we would find him in a stable, however. After we discovered there was no new prince at Herod's palace, we left. Again we saw the shining star but we became confused at the crossroads, not knowing which road to take. We asked some shepherds, watching the Temple sheep, if they had seen a star. They told us of seeing a bright star one night about a moon ago. They said that angels sang, and after following the star, they found a baby in a stable at the Bethlehem inn. We were delighted and mentioned that we would be returning soon as King Herod wanted to know more about the royal birth. He asked us to report where we found the new prince.

"The eldest of the three shepherds told us not to trust Herod, a mad man jealous of any threat to his throne; a man who had murdered his wife and his own sons."

Balthazar added, "Indeed we were grateful for his information as we had no idea—Herod was such a genial host, lavishing upon us a sumptuous feast in the company of his own wise men. Indeed it was a joy to talk with them and tell them of the prophecy. They urged us to stay but felt it necessary to hurry on as we were pressed to reach our destination."

"The shepherd was right," Joseph said. "Herod is a mad man. I would not trust him. He would feel no shame for decreeing your deaths after he heard from you again."

"Just as we thought, so we have decided to take an alternate route to our homeland," said the shortest of the three, dressed in priest's white, heavily trimmed with golden swirls about his waist. A tall turban, so close fitting it hid his hair, had a capelike cloth flowing freely from it, covering his shoulders. Over his forehead was centered a gold and silver disk engraved with radiating signs of the Zodiac.

"I am Melchoir," he said. "We are come bearing gifts to the newborn King. I leave this in honor of your royal birth." He placed a shining, small casket before the child and knelt saying, "Bless me, Messiah, that I may discover new ideas."

The one called Gaspar also knelt and said, "I give this in honor of your divinity. Messiah, bless me with greater wisdom to unravel knotty problems."

Balthazar placed his casket beside the others. " My gift honors death, that mysterious event of life which all people experience. My Lord, I pray you might insure my peace of mind."

"We are grateful to you and accept these in the spirit in which you give them, wise men." Mary said, bowing to than.

Overcome with the unexpected visitation, Joseph hesitated and then resumed his genial manner as host. "We were just packing to return to our home in Nazareth," he said. "Another day and you might have missed us."

"We would have found you," Balthazar assured him. "The shining star would have led us to Him, for it is written in the stars that this birth would be noted." The other two wise men nodded in agreement.

Melchoir said, "Now, we must leave. Our mission has been accomplished. We hasten our return so that we may chronicle this event for the future." The three ornately dressed men bowed low and left the stable.

Mary and Joseph were amazed at the grandeur of the men and their gifts. Neither had seen such magnificent boxes. Mary opened the first. Both of them gasped, "Gold!" Joseph ran his fingertips over the gleaming nuggets.

"This is a fortune, Mary," he said. "These will ensure Jesus' education with a fine rabbi . . . possibly at the Temple. We will keep it safe for his future. "

When Joseph lifted the lid of the second box a fragrance wafted about them. "Sweeter than the fragrance of the lilies when I met Gabriel," Mary said.

"It is frankincense," Joseph said. "At the Temple last year a very rich man offered it in sacrifice. I had never smelled such a rich odor and I inquired its name. I was told that it was a rare and extemely expensive perfume, imported across the Arabian desert."

Mary opened the last lid and shut it immediately.

"Myrrh," she said. "I will never forget using that anointing oil on Rebecca's body. Joseph, I know this is a warning of impending death. That old man and now this." She began to cry.

"That was just an old man's rumblings, Mary. Don't fret."

"No, there was something sincere about the old man's words—as if he had a soothsayer's ability to foresee the future. He knew the Son of God when he saw him. We did not tell him. He knew."

Then Joseph held her close to him. "It has been a difficult day for you, my little wife—glorious and sorrowful at the same time. But then, isn't life like that? We laugh some, and then we cry." He put his hand under her chin and lifted her tear-stained face. "The Lord and I will be with you and love you all the days of your life, Mary."

With tenderness he allayed her fears aroused by her encounters with Simeon and the golden box of myrrh. He cradled her in his arms, comforting her, and that night, for the first time, he knew her as his wife.

Chapter Twenty-two

The Flight to Egypt

"Egypt?" Mary asked. "Are you sure, Joseph?"

"Positive. We must hurry." Already he was pulling his robe about him. "I awakened after Gabriel spoke to me in a dream. Danger for Jesus lurks in Bethlehem. Herod is searching for the child to destroy him!" [1]

"The magi!" Mary hurried to the manger where the baby lay asleep. "Spies must have followed them. By now Herod knows they are returning to their homeland without stopping at the palace and, no doubt, he is in a rage. Yes. We must hurry!"

Mary gathered their few belongings, not already packed, while Joseph readied Jericho and Jezreel. Dawn had not yet lightened the sky when they reached the city gate. Mary and the animals huddled in the deepest shadows of the wall while Joseph fumbled with the gate lock, soundlessly lifting the heavy security-bar. He led his family out and closed the gate to keep their escape unnoticed.

"We must not be on the road from Jerusalem lest we meet Herod's men returning to Bethlehem," he said. "I think we should go by the way of Hebron. No one will look for us there, as it is more difficult to travel than the paved road through Gaza. I will ask directions from there."

"The Lord will protect us, Joseph. He will show us the way."

The winds were sharp and swept from deep crevices bits of snow which had not yet melted. Mary held Jesus close to her to protect him from the cold. She was thankful for the woolen blankets that she had made at Elizabeth's house. Even though the sky was midnight black, with only distant star-lights shimmering, the hard-packed, tan ribbon of stone was luminescent, highlighting the rocks and scrub vegetation along the way. Joseph walked ahead, watching for holes and boulders which might be dangerous for the animals. He led Jericho. Jezreel followed. Mary and Joseph went without speaking for fear their voices might reverberate against the rocky cliffs.

They were out of the sight of Bethlehem when the sun rose, spreading its warming rays. Feeling safer with the distance between them and Herod, Joseph mounted Jezreel and rode beside Mary.

"This isn't the direction we planned to be going this morning," Joseph said.

"No, it certainly isn't and I'm disappointed. I thought I would be seeing Elizabeth soon."

"When we return, we will visit her, I promise," Joseph said.

"But when will that be?"

"I have no idea. We will have to wait until it is safe. We'll know. I think your faith is wearing off on me, Mary. I expect Gabriel to speak to me again."

It was the sixth hour when the little family entered the village of Hebron, smaller than Bethlehem, and found a caravan pausing at the well. The men were watering their animals and talking route plans while the women and children moved about, visiting and munching on bread and cheese. Some boys were running around in circles, chasing each other and yelling. Mary and Joseph were accepted as part of the group, and learned the destination was Beersheba, a town on the border between Judea and the Roman province of Syria.

The trip from Hebron to Beersheba promised pleasant weather, a relief from the piercing winds of the mountain peaks. The caravan slowly descended to the valley where the "place of many wells" had grown into an important way station at the edge of the great desert. Here they could choose between two roads to Egypt: one directly south through the desert, the other to the west meeting the paved Via Maris, bordering the Mediterranean.

At the evening meal time Mary mingled among the other mothers who had babies or small children. She felt at home with this assorted group, made up of people very similar to those of the first caravan she rode in, the one on the way to Elizabeth's. Many women and children, riding on asses, were part of the parade which included the long train of pack-camels and other goods-bearing animals. Some families were migrating to new lands; others were accompanying husbands and fathers on buying and selling trips covering many Roman provinces.

Here Mary met Olga, the Egyptian. Olga was married to Demetrius, who made his living buying and selling whatever he found to be profitable. They had no children. Olga traveled beside her husband doing a man's work, riding herd on loaded camels, cracking the whip and calling out commands during the day. In the evenings she cherished even short visits with other women. She felt the lack of children as deeply as any Hebrew woman felt, as if she were not a whole person because she could not bear a child. Olga attached herself to Mary and Jesus.

"Take the road to the Via Maris," she advised. "That is a well traveled highway, and paved all the way to Memphis . . . and if you want to go to Alexandria you may take a boat down the river."

"I do not know where my husband has decided to go," Mary said.

"You are Hebrew, are you not?"

"Yes."

"Then, go to Heliopolis . . . some call it On. There are many of your people there. And you can see the pyramids on the other side of the river."

"Pyramids?" Mary asked.

"Monuments . . . burying places for our dead Pharaohs, our kings of centuries past. You have nothing like that in your country."

"We have a wonderful temple in Jerusalem!"

"I have seen it many times. It is quite impressive yet I can't for the life of me understand how you Hebrews can believe that only one god can serve everyone, being everywhere, doing everything. We have many gods who can divide up the tasks of helping us live. Demetrius has his set of Greek gods, and I have my own . . . Horus, Osiris, a whole sacred family to look after running this world and the next."

"Our one true God is hard to explain to one who has depended on graven images for gods, but you see, we worship the One True God who made this world and who supervises it now. I can't imagine praying to an idol god made of wood, stone, or metal. Ours is a spirit, and we are made in his image, so our Torah tells us."

"I've always admired you Jews. You are devoted to your Yahweh. You really believe, don't you.?"

"We do not speak that name. It is too sacred. Of course, I am devoted. I know my God lives." Mary picked up Jesus from his temporary bed which she had fashioned by folding her father's soft wool blanket many times. "How can you deny that a living god made this child possible?"

"I can't." Olga said, shaking her head. "Perhaps you will teach me something about your God. I feel that it would be good believing as you do, and yet I am afraid to abandon what I have been taught since I was a child. The anger of the gods is fearsome."

"I will try to show you that *Adonai* is a God of love. Is there a synagogue in this city . . . Heliopolis?"

"A fine one . . . and a university too."

"Do you think I could go there and learn how to read and write Greek? Even our Temple has Greek words I cannot understand."

"I shall be glad to acquaint you with an old priest of my temple. He is very learned and will feel it a privilege to teach you, I'm sure."

"It is my Lord's will that I learn," Mary said without explanation.

Olga and Mary parted, promising to visit the next day but the next day was one for which Mary was not prepared. The morning hours were pleasant, but the afternoon sun poured its rays down with no mercy. Mary saw many little oases of palm trees and lakes, only to have them disappear as the caravan lumbered on. Joseph explained that they were merely mirages, mysteries of the desert. Before the evening sun went down they reached a true oasis where a welling spring nurtured a thin stand of date palms. Surrounded by the wasteland of desert sand, they camped in the skimpy shade. Following the daily pattern the men worked with the animals and checked the cargoes while the women took care of the children and prepared the evening meal. Mary saw Olga at the well, working beside Demetrius. Several women with small children gathered around Mary, wanting to see the baby.

"Have you ever ridden through the desert before?" one of the mothers asked. "I think not. You have the child wrapped too warmly. Take off those swaddling bands and allow his feet and legs to be free to whatever breeze might blow. It is very hot here, and it gets worse."

"But what of his limbs? Won't they grow crooked?"

"Old wives tales, my dear. Look at my boy running," she pointed to a six-year old racing around in a circle, burning off energy he had stored during the long, tiresome, hot ride. "Do his legs look bowed? I didn't put the first band on that child."

"And he looks so joyful!" Mary said as she began to remove the white cloths she had kept wrapped around the tiny body since he was born. Jesus kicked and waved his arms around, gurgling with delighted freedom. That was the last time he was bound to the swaddling board. "Silly idea, anyway," she said.

After everyone had eaten and the cooking pots were cleaned, the women gathered as usual, to talk of families and food preparation. The men clustered in knots to exchange ideas of business, taxes, and the governments of many countries. Sudden bursts of laughter came as ribald jokes and stories were shared.

The children dropped asleep quickly, and one by one the crowd lay down on mats or cloaks to rest. It had been a long, hot ride through the arid land. The hour was late when Olga greeted Mary.

"We'll have to talk another time. I'm tired from watering and caring for the camels. Being a driver is hard at best. It's been a while since I drove over the sands and we still have a long way to go."

When the final darkness fell, the campers formed a quiet circle around the fire. In the distance the howling of wolves and the nerve shattering, laughing cry of hyenas pierced the emptiness of the desert wasteland. The men volunteered watch-times throughout the night while the families rested. Mary slept as soundly as Jesus, knowing they were being protected through the night.

Mary's throat was parched and her eyes ached from the glare of the sun reflecting the vast stretches of blinding, hot sand. When the caravan reached the paved road, the Via Maris which skirted the Great Sea, she welcomed the water cooled breezes. Spray-drenched palm trees and blooming plants bordering the brilliant blue waters created a welcome oasis along the shore. She longed to be as one of the children, running in circles with wild abandon over the hard-packed sand of the beach.

At the crossroads of the two roads was a bustling commercial community. Mary had never seen docks filled with ships where cargoes of fibers, dyes, metal pots, pottery, rugs, silks, perfumes, and wheat, were unload and carried away on laden camels. At the same time land shipments were lifted from laden camels and transferred to ships holds. She was thrilled with the excitement of the vast numbers of travelers moving about in this hub of transportation.

Olga saw Mary and left her animals briefly in order to greet her friend. "Mary, isn't this exciting? To think that all merchandise moving from north to south, from south to north pass through here. Of course, we have to remember that Via Maris is the road that invaders have used from the times of antiquity. Back and forth came the Romans, the Egyptians, the Grecians, the Hittite, and the Persians. Yes, all the peoples of the world have moved over this road."

"Indeed, Abraham moved his flock from the land of Dan to the fertile Nile to find pasture for his sheep and food for his people." Mary was overcome with the historical presence of long-forgotten heroes. "Thank you, Olga for guiding us this way." She hugged her friend.

"I must go now, Demetrius is calling me back to help him with the animals," Olga ran off and disappeared in the milling crowd.

After a night's rest from the long desert drive, members of the caravan formed groups heading for far-away destinations. An air of confusion settled over the area. There were more men parading around in short pleated skirts than Mary had ever seen: uniformed Romans soldiers carrying spears and shields, plus Egyptian and Greek traders. Women were robed in sheer loose-fitting gowns, shamelessly open up the sides. Slaves worked bare but for a small breech cloth. Mary had difficulty adjusting her strict training in the ways of the people of the south, who obviously had learned to cope with the hot weather.

Olga made certain Mary's little family was included with the travelers going south along the sea. As Mary gathered her things together she wished she had some way to tell her parents that she was going to Egypt. Egypt! Such a long way from Nazareth. No one in their families had ever ventured that far.

In the late afternoon she could not keep her anxiety quiet. "Joseph," she said. "My parents will be very worried when we do not return. Would you ask among the traders if any are going to Damascus by the way of Nazareth that I might send a message home?"

"In this confusion with so many camels and drivers, how could I know which one to ask?"

"Ask them all."

"All?"

"If you don't I will. I'm not afraid. Olga will help me, if I ask her."

"Olga is a heathen . . . and she acts like a man. I forbid you to be with her."

"She works very hard and is a good camel driver, but she does not talk like a camel-driver. After her hours of working with the camels in the caravan she needs a woman to talk to. She is a sensitive and lonely woman. I will not refuse her, my husband. I believe she wants to know about *Adonai*."

"She is a gentile. An unbeliever who worships idols. An abomination to our God!"

"She is a person made in the image of our God." Drawing herself up to her full height and lifting her chin, Mary said, "Let's not quarrel about Olga, my dear husband. What we are discussing is the finding of a merchant going through Nazareth. Remember?"

"You seem very certain we will find someone," Joseph said over his shoulder as he left.

"The Lord be with you, my Husband," she smiled as she called after him. "Just look for a man with a reed perched over his ear."

Mary was fascinated by the confusion. She saw many men writing bills for merchandise being loaded and unloaded. In the noisy din she thought she heard a young man calling out that he wrote in several languages. She walked over to watch him. He had just finished writing a listing of oils and perfumes being readied for a trip to Jerusalem. He looked like a he might be a Roman. His skin was swarthy and his hair shining black. To her he looked like a scholar. He was slight of build and gestured with graceful feminine movements. Of course, she decided, he might be from Greece as he wore a short pleated skirt similar to the other men from that area. Certainly the extreme hot weather made the attire more practical than the long sweeping robes which were worn in Judea.

When the scribe turned to call out again that he wrote in many languages Mary went to his side and said, "I wish to send a short message to my parents. You write in Aramaic?"

The young man nodded and spread out his board, ink, and papyrus ready to take down her words.

"Dear Family," she began. "Baby Jesus, was born. Our trip home has been delayed, we know not how long. We are well. Love to all, Mary."

The scribe carefully penned the words, and sealed the papyrus roll with wax before he gave it to Mary. She paid him with some of the dinars she had received at her betrothal. He took the small roll from her hand and refused them.

"Those coins are of no value here," he said. "You will have to find a money-changer."

"My husband has Roman coins, but he is not here."

"Find him. I will wait."

Mary saw Joseph talking with an Arab. They both talked at the same time, waving their arms up and down then out. At last Joseph dropped a gold coin in the merchant's hand and the two men clasped each other on the shoulders, and kissed each cheek. He turned and saw Mary.

"Abou will take a message for you. He knows Nathan, the merchant of Nazareth, and he will take it to him."

Abou bowed low. "It will be a pleasure, my lady," he said.

"I already have the message finished. The young scribe over there has finished it but he refuses my dinars," Mary said. "I need Roman money to pay him."

"A wise young man, indeed." Abou nodded and smiled.

Chapter Twenty-three

The Journey s End

The camels seemed to sense that the end of the journey was near. Perhaps they smelled the dampness of the Nile or perhaps their drivers pressed them into moving faster. The caravan which had listlessly plodded through the extreme sun-scorched desert air now picked up speed. Jericho and Jezreel fell behind the swift, long-legged camels as the golden light of sunset washed over a distant city.

Riding an ass she had traded for a camel, Olga came up beside Mary, pointed toward the west and she called out, "That is Heliopolis."

Mary felt at home when she came into the city where the square white houses looked much like the ones in Nazareth. All along the way she had seen only round hut-like shelters, made of poles with palm-thatched conical roofs. It had all seemed like such an alien land with only palm trees for shade. But the narrow, walled-in and cobbled streets filled with people, camels and asses burdened with merchandise, offered the same excitement for Mary that Jerusalem had. Packs of yellow curs roamed the streets, devouring garbage thrown from the houses, barked and threatened the riders and rival dogs. Jericho shied at the snappings but Jezreel ignored them and continued to joggle Joseph through the dingy streets.

As Olga led the way through the noisy maze, she shouted to Mary, "I want to be sure your little family finds shelter among your people. I know that you will be happier with your own kind."

"Please don't go to a lot of bother for us," Mary protested. "We will be happy anywhere."

"We Egyptians are hospitable," Olga reached out and touched Mary's shoulder. "I see that you have decided to dress more sensibly."

Mary laughed. "The sun and the sand of this journey convinced me!"

Indeed, Mary had doffed many of her inner garments which she had needed for warmth in the mountains. A pale-blue linen shift replaced the woolen robe she had worn when she began her journey. However, she knew that she would never adapt to the fashion of Egyptian women: the knee length tight or pleated skirts, bare shoulders above breast-flattening bodices, hair cut to hang straight to the shoulders or heads shaved for wigs.

Mary had bound up her tresses with a ribbon and pinned it to the crown of her head for coolness. That morning when she had twisted the long strands of her golden hair into a coil, she thought of her mother with the heavy knot at the nape of her neck. Had her mother ever worn her hair loose about her shoulders? Mary had never been curious about her mother's girlhood, but lately, as she had ridden over the seemingly endless sand her mind had asked questions that she could not answer.

She promised herself that when she returned to Nazareth she would visit and talk more about the past; she would listen closely to all the stories her parents had to tell—stories she had listened to patiently, all the while eager to go out with her own friends. Up until now the remembering had all been rote, recalling ancestral names. Now Mary felt the need to know how her parents lived and felt as children.

She looked over at Joseph and smiled. He had refused to bend to the cooling freedom of Egyptian dress. His long woolen robe clung about his body and perspiration ran beneath his tight turban forming little rivulets to drip from his crisp black beard.

Olga's shrewd bargaining and her familiarity with the narrow streets found a home for her new friends among the craftsmen where the families were as poor as Mary and Joseph.

Joseph left each morning, carrying his tools, full of hope that he would find a day's labor for a few coins. When he did find work he soon discovered that joiners were considered no more valuable than slaves working in the muck of the Nile overflow. Skillful creativity was not rewarded by premium pay. In the building crafts only architects and engineers were acclaimed.

"I like the system in Judea better," he said. "There the skill of an artisan is appreciated. Here it is taken for granted. We work for a pittance—no higher than untrained brick makers!"

"But your skilled hands will feed us, my Husband. We must be grateful that you are able to work even in this oppressive heat. Every minute the prayer is within my heart that our stay here will be short."

The End

CHARACTERS

* Identifies the Biblical characters who participate in the events included in this novel.
\# Marks those names which have been accepted by tradition as participants.

Anna#	Mother of Mary, revered as St.Anna
Anna*	Prophetess at the Temple
Balthazar#	One of the Magi
Benjamin	Wealthy rug merchant of Nazareth
David	Younger brother of Mary
Elizabeth*	Mary's elderly cousin, wife of Zechariah, and mother of John the Baptist
Esther	Wife of the Bethlehem innkeeper
Gabriel*	Angel who appeared to Zechariah, Elizabeth, Mary and Joseph
Gaspar#	One of the Magi
Ishmael	Father of family who made Mary's trip to Elizabeth's possible
Jacob*	Father of Joseph
Jesus*	Son of the Virgin Mary
Joachim#	Father of Mary, husband of Anna
Jonathan	Young brother of Mary
John*	Son of Elizabeth and Zechariah
Joseph*	Husband of Mary
Josie	Wife of Levi, Anna's close friend
Laban	Rebecca's lover
Levi	Friend of Mary's parents
Mary*	Heroine of this book, Virgin, Mother of Jesus, wife of Joseph
Melchoir#	One of the Magi

Nadia   One of Elizabeth's Servants
Naomi   Daughter of Josie and Levi
Nathan   Wealthy merchant, Rebecca's father
Olga   Egyptian woman who befriends Mary
Rachel   Wife of Ishmael
Rebecca   Mary's friend, betrothed toBenjamin, stoned to
               death
Rhodia   Nadia's sister, Elizabeth's servant
Ruth   Deceased mother of Joseph
Salome*   Sister of Virgin Mary
Sarah   Midwife who attended Mary in the stable
Shammah   Innkeeper at Bethlehem
Simeon*   Aged man in the Temple who recognized the baby
               Jesus as the Messiah
Taddy   Boy shepherd who came to the stable
Uria   Youthful shepherd
Zechariah*   Husband to Elizabeth, father of John (The Baptist),
               brother of Joachim

                    The Faithful Animals
Jericho   Joseph's gift burro to Mary
Jezreel   Joseph's burro

HISTORICAL NAME

King Herod*, the Great, rebuilt the second Temple in Jerusalem to replace the one destroyed by invaders. Infamous for his slaughter of all boy babies after he learned of the birth of the "King of the Jews."

NOTES

Unless noted elsewhere, all quotations are from the *Holy Bible, Revised Standard Version,* however these quotations are interchangeable with *The New American Bible, Saint Joseph Edition*, Catholic Biblical Association of America.

Chapter 1
   1. Deuteronomy 22:23
Chapter 2
   1. Deuteronomy 6:4-9
Chapter 3
   1. Luke 1:28-37
   2. Luke 1:38
Chapter 4
   1. Psalms 145:1-3 *The New American Bible, Saint Joseph Edition*
   2. Edgar Cayce's *Story of Jesus* pp.127-128
   3. *Sabbath and Festival Prayer Book*, the Rabbinical Assembly of America and the United Synagogues of America, p.49
   4. Jonah 1:1
Chapter 5
   1. *Prayers, Blessings and Hymns* p.57
Chapter 9
   1. Luke 1:42-45
   2. Luke 1:46-55
   3. Luke 1:20
Chapter 11
   1. Matthew 1:18
Chapter 12
   1. Matthew 1:20-21

Chapter 15
1. Isaiah 7:14
2. *Everyday Life in the New Testament Times* p.146
3. Edgar Cayce's *Story of Jesus* p.128 and
Protevangelion, Ch.XVI:16f Lost Books of the Bible, p.36
Chapter 16
1. Micah 5:2
Chapter 17
1. Genesis 35:19-20
Chapter 18
1. Luke 2:14
Chapter 19
1. Luke 2:29-32
2. *Reader's Digest Story of the Bible World, page 137.*
Pleasantville NY., 1959
3. Luke 2:34-35
Chapter 20
1. Luke 2:24
Chapter 21
1. Matthew 2:1-12
Chapter 22
1. Matthew 2:13

BIBLIOGRAPHY

Asch, Sholen. *Mary.* N.Y.: G. P. Putnam's Sons. 1949.

Asimov, Isaac. *Asimov's Guide to the Bible.* N.Y.: Doubleday. 1968.

Barclay, William. *Jesus of Nazareth.* Nashville: Thomas Nelson. 1981

Barker, William P. *Everyone in the Bible.* Old Tappan, N.J.: Fleming H. Revell Co. 1966.

Battle, Gerald. *Armed with Love-Stories of the Disciples.* Nashville: Abingdon Press. 1973.

Beers, V. Gilbert: *The Victor Handbook of Bible Knowledge* USA: Victor Books. 1981

Benet, William Rose, Ed. *The Reader's Encyclopedia Vol. II* N.Y.: Thomas Y. Crowell Co. 1965

Bishop, Jim. *The Day Christ Died.* N.Y.: Harper & Bros. 1957; *The Day Christ was Born.* N.Y.: Harper & Bros. 1959

Bouquet, A. C. *Everyday Life in New Testament Times.* N.Y.: Charles Scribner. 1953

Brecher, Rabbi Ch. M., Ed. *Prayers, Blessings and Hymns.* N.Y.: Ktav Publishing House, Inc. 1960

Burrows, Millar. *The Dead Sea Scrolls.* N.Y.: The Viking Press. 1961

Caldwell, Taylor. *Judas.* N.Y. New American Library, Signet Book. 1978

Casson, Lionel. *Treasures of the World, The Pharaohs.* Chicago: Stonehenge Press, Inc. 1981

Central Conference of American Rabbis. *Gates of Prayer, New Union Prayer Book.* N.Y.: 1975

Crane, Dr. Frank, Ed. *The Lost Books of the Bible and the Forgotten Books of Eden.* N.Y.: Meridian Press, World Publishing. 1927

Cutler, Daniel S. *The Bible Cookbook*. N.Y.: William Morrow and Company, Inc. 1985

Daniel Raps, Henri. *Jesus and His Times*. N.Y.: E. P. Dutton, trans. 1954; *Daily Life in the Times of Jesus*. N.Y.: Hawthorne Books, Inc. trans. 1963

Davies, A. Powell. *The Meaning of the Dead Sea Scrolls*. N.Y.: New American Library. 1956

Deen, Edith. *All the Women of the Bible*. N.Y.: Harper and Row. 1955

Fosdick, Harry Emerson. *The Man from Nazareth*. N.Y.: Harper Bros. 1949

Friedlande, M. and Lady Magnus. *Outlines of Jewish History*. Philadelphia: Jewish Publication Society of America. 1890

Furst, Jeffrey, Ed. *Edgar Cayce's Story of Jesus*. N.Y.: Coward-McCann, Inc. 1968

Goodman, Naomi, Robert Marcus, Susan Woolhandler. *The Good Cookbook*. N.Y.: Dodd Mead & Company. 1986

Gordon, Cyrus H. *The World of the Old Testament*. Garden City: Doubleday & Co. 1958

Grant, Michael. *Jesus, An Historian's View of the Gospels*. N.Y.: Charles Scribner's Sons. 1977. History of Ancient Israel. N.Y. Charles Scribner's Sons. 1984

Greenfeld, Howard. *Passover*. N.Y.; Holt, Rinehart and Winston. 1978

Grisewood, John, Ed. *The Book of the Bible*. N.Y.: Golden Press. 1972

Harmon, Nolan B. Ed. *The Interpreter's Bible*. Nashville: Abingdon Press. 1953

Hastings, James, Ed. *Dictionary of the Bible*. N.Y.: Scribe's Sons. 1918

Heller, Abraham Mayer. *The Jew and His World*. N.Y.: Wayne Publishers, Inc. 196

Hertzberg, Arthur, Ed. *Judaism*. N.Y.: George Braziller. 1962

Holmes, Marjorie. *Two from Galilee*. Old Tappan, N. J.: Fleming H. Resell Co. 1973; *Three from Galilee*. N.Y.: Harper & Row. 1985

Holy Bible-Authorized King James Version. Chicago: Good
    Counsel Publishers. 1965
Holy Bible-Revised Standard Version. N.Y.: Thomas Nelson &
    Sons. 1952
Isaacson, Dr. Ben. *Dictionary of the Jewish Religion.* Englewood,
    N. J.: SBS Publishing Co. 1979
Keyes, Nelson Beecher. *Reader's Digest Story of the Bible World.*
    Pleasantville, N.Y.: Readers' Digest. 1959
La Croix, *Mary The Remnant.* N.Y.: Avon. 1981
Laymon, Charles M., Ed. *The Interpreter's One Volume
    Commentary On the Bible.* Nashville: Abindon Press. 1971
Lockyer, Herbert. *All the Men of the Bible.* Grand Rapids:
    Zondervan Publishing House. 1958
Lofts, Nora. *How Far to Bethlehem.* Garden City: Doubleday and
    Co. 1964
Mackie, George M. *Bible Manners and Customs.* Old Tappan:
    Fleming H. Revell Co. ND
Mathews, Basil. *A Life of Jesus.* N.Y. Richard Smith, Inc. 1931
Morton, H. V. and Rene Burri. *In Search of the Holy Land.* N.Y.:
    Dodd, Meade & Co. 1979
Muggeridge, Malcolm. *Jesus.* N.Y.: Harper & Row. 1975
O'Boyle, Patrick Cardinal, D.D. Imprim *The New American Bible -
    Saint Joseph Edition.* N.Y.: Catholic Book Publishing Co.
    1980
Oursler, Fulton. *Greatest Story Ever Told.* Garden City: Image
    Books, Doubleday & Co. 1961
Packer, James I., Merrill C. Tenner, and William White. *The Land
    of the Bible.* Nashville: Thomas Nelson. 1980
Radin, Max. *The Life of the People in Biblical Times.* Philadelphia:
    Jewish Publication Society. 1943
Rhymer, Joseph. *Atlas of the Biblical World.* N.Y.: Greenwich
    House. 1982
Rogerson, John. *Atlas of the Bible.* Oxford: Equinox. 1985
Ross, Bette M. *The Thirteenth Disciple.* Old Tappan, N. J. Fleming
    H. Revell Co. 1984
Shanks, Hershel, Ed. *Recent Archaeology in the Land of Israel.*
    Washington, D. C.: Biblical Archaeology Society. 1984

Sheen, Fulton J. *Life of Christ*. N.Y.: McGraw-Hill Book Company. 1958

Silverman, Rabbi Morris, Ed. *Sabbath and Festival Prayer Book*. USA: Rabbinical Assembly of America and the United Synagogues of America. 1983

Slaughter, Frank G. *The Galileans*. N.Y.: Doubleday Co. 1957

Smith, Wm. Robertson, Ed. *Encyclopedia Britannica, Ninth Edition*. Edinburgh: Black Publishers. 1891

Steinsaltz, Adin. *The Essential Talmud*. N.Y.: Basic Books, Inc. 1976

Wagenknecht, Edward. *The Story of Jesus in World Literature*. N.Y.: Creative Age Press, Inc. 1946

Walker, Winifred. *All the Plants of the Bible*. Garden City: Doubleday & Co., Inc. 1979

Walton, Robert C., Ed. *A Source Book of the Bible for Teachers*. Camden, N.J.: Thomas Nelson, Inc. 1970

Whiston, William. Trans. *The Works of Josephus*. N.Y.: John B. Alden Publisher. 1884

Wouk, Herman. *This is my God*. N.Y. Doubleday & Co. 1959

Young, Robert, Ed. *Analytical Concordance to the Bible*. N.Y.: Funk & Wagnall's Co. ND

Whiston, William. Trans. *The Works of Josephus*. N.Y.: John B. Alden Publisher. 1884